MURDER CITY

by

L.J. LAURA

First paperback edition February 2020

ISBN: 9781675555446

Dedication

I want to thank my mother for instilling this quality in me when I didn't even know I had it.

I want to thank my children for giving me a reason to pursue writing. I wanted to be there for them when I wasn't physically able due to my poor decision making at the time.

I want to thank my sister Jazmyn for just being herself and allowing me to stay with her when I was in Detroit. I want to thank my sister Rayna who is always there to support me through my ups and downs and gave me a clear head when my judgement was cloudy. You are a big inspiration to me and such a wonderful person at heart I couldn't ask for a better angel, not only in my life but my families.

I want to thank my wife for having my back and holding me down at my lowest times. Thank you for loving me and being there for me, even when you didn't have to. Thank you for being a great parent, teacher, and the most helping wife a man can ask for.

I love each and every one of you. Thank you all for being there for me when I needed you the most.

In Loving Memory
Of
Dontaya "Smakks" Johnson

My brother for life, continue to watch over us all. Rest in Paradise.

MURDER CITY

1

It was the beginning of December in Detroit. Three friends were headed back to their spot after looking for a lick to hit. The day was a bust, they came up empty handed, if it wasn't for the gas tank being on E, they would still be on a mission.

"Sit back, sit back" Scoop said, "The police behind us. Don't make any sudden moves. Just play it cool."

"If they pull us over, I'm gone spray their car up" Said Supreme. "What the fuck are you talking about, we ridin on fumes, aint no way we gone get away" Justice said. "Yall both just chill, when the light turns green, we'll see what they are going to do" spoke Scoop. Supreme   clutched on the TEC-9 that was in his lap and waited for the lights to flash behind them. The light turned green, and Scoop pushed down on the gas and pulled through the intersection.

The lights came on and the siren sounded, Scoop began to change lanes and pull over as Supreme and Justice both were holding their guns ready to open fire, but the police car flew past them.

Supreme and Justice let out a long breath of relief. Scoop wasn't shook up at all, he reached into the ash tray and lit his half of Newport had left. "Never make a move like that unless it's your final option." Scoop passed the butt end of the cigarette to Supreme as he made a right turn onto Winthrop and headed to the spot. Just as they were pulling into the driveway the car died. They grabbed the guns and headed into the house. "Fuck, we need some money. I'm tired of being broke, and every lick we hit only brings us back to the same spot. This shit like living paycheck to paycheck. We can't even buy a box of Newport's, let alone bottles and blunts." Supreme said.

"What the fuck you know about paycheck to paycheck? You aint never had a job. Look we got to make something shake, rents due in a few days, the power bill is past due, and the gas about to get cut off" Justice said. "That's what I'm talking about" Supreme said.

"Yall both need to calm down, we gone come up with something, but right now we need to chill and smoke something." Scoop said. "Oh, yeah and where we gone get some weed from?" "I already got that under control, Katrina is on her way over and she gone bring a bottle and some weed. Stop being so negative all the time" Scoop said.

The doorbell rang a few minutes later and Katrina walked in with her Manolos on, and her ass shaking looking good like always. Supreme and Justice couldn't understand how Scoop kept this dime piece around, she would move and do what he said at the drop of a dime, and he was broke just like them.

Katrina gave Scoop a kiss and he slapped her on the ass. They all sat in the living room around the table talking as she pulled out the bottle of Paul Masson and a few red cups. She dug her hand into her bra, and she pulled out an eighth of some O.G Kush and a fifty-dollar bill and handed it to Scoop. They all poured a cup of drank as Scoop rolled a few blunts. After Justice and Supreme got some weed and alcohol in their system they began to talk about their next plan, but Katrina over heard them. She looked at Scoop as she sat in his lap. "Baby is everything okay?" "Yeah, why you ask that?" "be real with me, you know I'm always real with you." "Yeah, I know, and I respect you for that." He paused and began to speak again "look, we behind on everything. We took a lost and been trying to bounce back, but aint shit fell through. So, we trying to find a lick to hit to set things straight."

Katrina gave Scoop a kiss and leaned back to look him in the eyes "why don't you hustle baby?" "That's already on my agenda when I catch these bills up, and I get my hands on some work. We gotta make something happen fast, I refuse to be on my ass."

She smiled and said, "I got a lick for you and your boys to hit baby, and I know it will be worth it" "oh, yeah?' "Yeah, this nigga I met at the strip club been trying to get at me, and he always flashing his money, jewelry, and talking about his cars. But I just make him spend the money in the club. I never been to his spot or anything, and he always trying to pay me for some pussy. I know I can get all the info you need to hit the lick." She said.

"So, what do you want out of this?" "If I wanted anything but you, would I be over here spending and giving my money to you. Or letting you in this pussy?" Scoop laughed at her comment and kissed her on the cheek. She got up off his lap and grabbed him by his hand, and they walked to his room in the back, while Supreme and Justice refilled their cups full of Paul Masson and got tipsy.

2

Scoop woke up bright and early to some head. It calmed his morning wood, and he was ready for the day. Katrina got dressed and took her toothbrush out her purse and went to the bathroom to bush her teeth. She gave scoop a kiss, "I got a few things to do baby, but I will call you later. I'm gone check on that thang and try to put everything together. So, make sure you answer the phone when I call." "I got you ma." Scoop slapped her on the booty as she walked out the door. "Make sure you keep it tight for me." "You know I will" she said and slid into her Dodge Charger and pulled off into the winter snow.

Scoop locked the door, walked into the living room, sat down, and rolled up a blunt. Justice and

Supreme was still sleep, so scoop turned on the radio and lit the blunt.

The base came through the speakers and Supreme jumped up and fell on the floor. "What the fuck bruh?" Scoop handed him the blunt. He took it and took a deep breath of the Kush smoke and calmed his nerves.

Justice woke up to the smell of weed. He rubbed his eyes and sat up. His gun was in his hand, so he sat it on the table. He was prepared for anything, he always held his gun close, and ready for whatever. Supreme passed the blunt to Justice "see this how we supposed to be living. Wake and bake, and pussy on the plate, every day."

"Look Katrina said she got a lick for us to hit, but she gotta put it together. So, until then we gotta go get it ourselves, tomorrow is the last payment day for the lights, so let's get ourselves together and get to the money." Scoop said.

They all hit the shower one after the other and got their self together. They all wore black and got strapped up. Justice had got ten dollars from Scoop and went next door to ask the neighbor for a ride to the gas station to fill up the gas can. When he got back they were ready to go. They pulled up to the gas station and got ten more dollars in gas, a pack of Newport 100s and they headed toward Grand River.

This was a neighborhood they really didn't get

along with due to previous encounters from the past. They decided to roll through and try to catch a corner hustler and jump out on him.

"Look out Scoop, ain't shit moving over here. Let's head over toward Plymouth and Greenfield, that's where all the smokers coping from." Justice said. "Yeah, lets slide through there and see if anything going on over there." Supreme chimed in.

About fifteen minutes later they were making a right onto Plymouth, they made another right on Mettatal and as soon as they hit the residential street they spotted a fiend buying a rock from someone standing next to the stop sign up ahead.

Supreme gripped the TEC-9 "Justice get ready, we gone jump out on him." Scoop pulled up to the stop sign and the two doors flew open. "Get yo bitch ass on the ground" Supreme said as he smacked him in the face with the Tec. He fell onto the ground as the fiend took off running down the street. Blood dripped from over his right eye.

Justice felt around his waist band and pulled a 9mm from off his hip and ran through his pockets. "Come on man don't do this to me, this all I got. My kids gotta eat." "I gotta eat too,and rents due bitch." Supreme said. "We like Robin Hood, takin from the niggas that have, and keepin for our needs" Justice said as he pulled a decent stack of money from out of the guys Timberland boots.

7

"Where the dope at?' Scoop yelled out the car as he waited patiently for his boys to get everything off the dude laying on the ground.

Justice pressed his Glock to his forehead "Where the dope at bitch?' He said in a smooth and calm tone. "That was the last of it, I don't have anymore" he said.

Supreme spoke up "I'm gone dead this cornball right here" he cocked the Tec -9 and slowly squeezed the trigger "wait, wait, ok, ok, ok he cried as he stuck his hand between his butt cheeks and pulled out a sandwich bag full of crack. "This all I got," Justice snatched the dope out his hand and slapped him with his Glock, "That's for lying, now get your bum ass up and shake the spot before I get to squeezing." Supreme said. He got off the ground and started to jog down the street holding his eye.

Supreme and Justice slid back into the ride and Scoop pulled off and made a right at the stop sign and sped down the residential street toward Greenfield.

Justice tossed the dope upfront into Supremes lap, and started counting the money they peeled from ol'boy. "How much did he have?" Scoop asked as he turned onto Greenfield. "Eleven hundred and thirty dollars" he said with a smirk on his face, "plus the dope we got." "Bust it down three ways" Justice said. "I'm gone say its three hundred and seventy-five each with five dollars left, so here's three hundred and seventy each and we gone use these twenty dollars for gas." "I'm good with that" "me too" said Scoop and Supreme.

"We gone slide over to my aunt house and see if we can get off that work over there, and get off the street for a second," Scoop said. He sparked a Newport and gave the box to his boys, so they could calm their nerves too.

3

Katrina pulled up to the club earlier than usual, she seen Dunks car in the parking lot and smiled. She didn't have any intention on working today so she decided to play her cards right.

She walked into the club and Dunk had two females in front of him dancing. Katrina walked right past him throwing her ass back and forth as she headed to the dressing room. Dunk spotted her and tried to keep his composure, but the two chicks dancing in front of him sensed his attention shifting. He was thinking about what he could say to get her to go out with him, so he threw a couple more dollars and told them he would holla at them later.

Katrina grabbed her extra work bag out her locker and talked to a couple of the other girls to waste time. She got herself together and walked back onto the floor and headed toward the door. Before she could make it out Dunk bee-lined from the bar and grabbed her hand as she walked toward the door. "Hold up ma, let me holla at you real quick," "What is it now? Do you have something to tell me, or is it the same shit?"

"I got a lot to say. Can we go have lunch?" "Time is money Dunk and I'm in the middle of something." "Look" he said as he pulled out a stack of hundred-dollar bills, he counted out a thousand dollars and put it in her hand, "can we have lunch and you can go on about your business after we talk over a meal."

She put the money in her bra, "where are you trying to go?" "Somewhere simple. TGIF off ten mile." "I'll follow you there, and once we get there you have an hour," "that's a bet" he said.

They got into their vehicles and Dunk grabbed his nutts thinking "finally." He pulled off in his new Jaguar XF with Katrina tailing him as they headed toward Fridays.

They got a booth and ordered drinks. "Why did it take so much time and effort for me to have a one on one outside of the club with you?" "I know you are a guy who likes to show off, and your egos out the roof and I usually don't bother with your type. I honestly don't think you know how to treat a woman." "So, you think I'm an asshole, right?" "I guess you can say that." "Well how can I change how you look at me?" "by being yourself and stop being so egocentric. You know how I see it?" "What's that?" "If you had a woman you would only want to receive pussy and head from her and wouldn't want to give any in return." Katrina said.

"I guess you think you know me..." "I just know your type, that's all." Dunk took a sip of his vodka, "how much do you think you know me, or my type?" "Very well. I know you couldn't satisfy me" she said with a laugh as she finished her mimosa. She motioned for the waitress to bring her another drink. "I believe I could, if given the chance." "So, your good with your tongue? I don't see you being a man of that nature." "Well let's find out, let me take you to the Ramada?"

She started laughing so loud everyone started looking at them. "sorry boo boo, but I don't do motels, hotels or Holiday Inns. If I don't deserve to be in your bed you don't deserve a taste of this chocolate cherry."

Dunk couldn't let her slip through his fingers when he was so close to getting what he wanted. He pulled out a fifty-dollar bill from his pocket and placed it on the table. "Follow me" he said as he got up from the table.

Katrina pulled behind Dunk as they made turn after turn. Ten minutes later they pulled into the driveway of a nice house in a nice neighborhood. There were several other cars in his driveway, Dunk hit the garage door opener and inside sat a BMW M6 drop top, a BMW 750 LI, and a Range Rove. He got out the car, and motioned for Katrina to come in. She got out of her car and walked into the garage and it closed behind her. She looked at the cars and kind of smiled and continued to follow him into the house.

"This nigga got to really be getting some bread, all these cars, and a nice house" she thought. They walked past the kitchen, through the living room and the up the stairs toward his bedroom. His place was laced, a straight bachelors pad.

They walked into his room and there were mirrors everywhere, there was a stripper pole in the corner and a black chair sitting close to it. Dunk took off his leather Gucci jacket and walked toward his walk-in closet and placed it on the door hook.

When he came back from his closet Katrina was sitting on the bed with her jacket and heels off. Her button was undone to her guess jeans. She began to pull them down as he walked over to her. She came all the way out of her pants and grabbed Dunk by his hand and pulled him down onto his knees and he slid her panties to the side and licked from her asshole to her clit.

Katrina laid back as he began to flick his tongue back and forth and sucked on her with great passion. He slid his tongue inside her pussy and ate her like an entree. She sat up after a few minutes and made him lay on the bed and straddled his face. She began to ride his tongue.

A few minutes later she began to cum. She grabbed Dunk by his head and pushed her pussy down on his face in a back and forth motion and squirted her juices all over him.

She got up and reached into her purse and pulled out a wet wipe and wiped herself. She fixed her panties and put her jeans back on. "Hold up, hold up, hold up. You ain't gone give me no pussy after I just put my mouth all on it?" She laughed, "that wasn't a part of the agreement, and we've been gone longer than an hour." She put her heels and her jacket on and grabbed her purse.

"You gone walk me to the door?" Dunk couldn't believe what was going on. This never happened to him, but he couldn't get out of character now. No, he was smarter than that. He still wanted the pussy, especially after he got a taste of it.

"Look, I got five grand if you let me hit that pussy ma." "I gotta go," "Don't act like you don't want the money" "Yeah, I want the money, but I have to go. Why don't you give me your number and I'll take you up on that offer later?" She said.

"I gave you my card like ten times." "Well one more time won't hurt." She put his number in her phone and walked out the door. "So, how was I pleasing you?' She turned back and said, "you were ok," and smiled. She got into her car and pulled out the driveway and drove off. Checkmate!

4

coop, Supreme and Justice walked into Scoops aunts house on the corner of 12ᵗʰ street and Hazelwood. This area was known for drugs, and a lot of murderers, but in their minds, death was worth the risk of trying to get rich. Some would say "Get Rich or Die Trying."

"What's going on nephew" Mary said greeting all three of them. "Shit, just coming to check on you, and see if you wanted to do a little business." "What kind of business you are talking about?" She said. Supreme pulled the dope out his coat pocket and tossed it to Mary. She eyed the bag, "why this bag smell like shit?' she asked. They all broke out laughing. "Supreme said because it is the shit."

"Yall follow me to the kitchen." They all sat at the table. Mary pulled open a drawer and grabbed a digital scale and placed it on the table next to Supreme and Justice. The bag of dope was dropped on the scale and the number read 15.5g.

"How much yall want for this?' "A half ounce goes for eight hundred and fifty, but we'll take seven hundred and fifty" and you can keep the extra half gram" Justice said. "Well how do I know if it's any good?" "Look aunt Mary, when do I ever bring you anything bad?" She thought about what he said and dug into her bra and pulled out a decent stack of money and counted "five hundred, six hundred, seven hundred, seven hundred and fifty." She dropped the money on the table, Justice split the money down in three ways, as Scoop lit a Newport.

"So, what's been going on around here auntie?" Have you seen my mom?" "I haven't seen Deana in about three weeks. She around here somewhere doing her thang." How was she when you see her?" "She looked good, said she had a place over on Palestine behind the old Fisher building. "That's good." "How have yall been?" she said. "Shit, you know we hanging in there, gettin it how we live" Supreme said. "Yeah, we been good" Scoop said.

"Look, we been thinking about going big, but don't have and clients and I wanted to talk to you about that." "Oh, yeah!" "Yeah, so if we get our hands on some work, are you willing to help set us up? I don't want to step on your toes at all, but I know you've been doing this a long time and know a lot of people."

"I'm willing to help yall out, but under one condition." "What's that?" Justice asked as he exhaled cigarette smoke. "Give me a better deal than my connect right now, and we will be helping each other. You know, scratch my back and I scratch yours."

There was a knock at the door and Mary left them sitting in the kitchen as she went to tend to her business. She came walking back with a fade. "Kim these are my nephews, guys this is Kim." Kim was a fine yellow bone with a nice ass, and pretty smile. Her appearance was good and she had all her teeth.

Mary handed her two rocks from the bag she got from her nephews and they walked back to the living room and had a few words, then she left. Justice asked, "aunt Mary, she smokes dope?" "Nah she comes to buy for her mom. She takes care of her and tries to keep her out the streets, and so far, she's been doing a good job." Said Mary.

"I think I'm in love!" Justice said "stop lying, you just want to fuck" said Supreme, and Scoop laughed. "Put in a word for me auntie." Justice said. As soon as Scoop got ready to say something his phone started to vibrate and killed his train of thought when he looked at his screen.

It was a text message from Katrina that read "its good tonight, so be ready. Imma give you the address and when I text you again later tonight I want you to call me, and ill fill you in." he texted back "bet, that!"

"Aunt Mary you got a deal, if we go big we will look out, and you do that for us too." Scoop said as he placed his phone back into his pocket. Mary shook all of their hands and kissed them on the cheek."

Scoop stood up "well, we gotta go make a few moves Justice and Supreme stood up in Unisom and they headed toward the door. "Make sure you tell Kim about me "Justice said with a smile on his face as he hugged her and headed to the car.

When they all got into the car Supreme spoke "what's the deal bruh? What's going on?' "The lick is a go tonight, so we gotta be ready. Katrina gone call me in a little bit to run down the info" Scoop said as they pulled onto Rosa Parks St.

5

8'oclock came around fast, and Scoop and his boys were sitting in a stolen Jeep Cherokee down the street from Dunks house waiting for a text from Katrina.

"How much money and dope you think he got in there?" Justice said. "He gotta have a nice amount staying out here in a house like that. This nigga got the new Jag, and a Range Rover in his driveway" said Supreme.

The text message came through to Scoops phone "come now" Scoop pulled into the driveway with the lights off and the garage door opened. They pulled on their masks and walked into the garage.

They all looked at the cars in the garage and knew this was going to be a big hit. Supreme led the way gripping his Glock-17 with a silencer on it.

Supreme, Scoop and Justice swept the first floor and came up clean. They crept up the stairs and halfway up they heard the music coming out the bedroom. They split up to clear the rest of the house to make sure no one else was there.

Supreme went for the room playing the music, and as he crept in he saw a man on his knees with his head between Katrina's thighs. He tried to tip toe over behind him, but Dunk seen the movement out the corner of his eye and reached for his gun on the nightstand. Supreme pulled the trigger twice sending a bullet through his shoulder and the other grazed his head.

Dunk let out a yell as he knocked over the nightstand. Katrina pulled back to the other side of the bed and started to put her clothes back on.

Supreme ran over to him and slapped him in the head with the pistol knocking him out, just as Scoop and Justice rushed into the room.

Supreme and Scoop taped Dunks arms behind his back and laid him on the bed. "I think the safe is in the closet" Katrina said. Justice walked through the bathroom and into the walk-in closet and there stood a five-foot iron cast safe with a digital keypad.

"It's right here, but its locked" Justice said. He tried to push the safe, but it wouldn't budge. "This bitch gotta weight a thousand pounds he thought to himself.

Scoop made his way to the closet, "I don't know how we gone get that bitch down the stairs." "We make him give us the code" Scoop said.

When they came back to the bed Scoop had a piece of tape on Dunks mouth. "Get me a glass of water Katrina." She came back, and Scoop threw the water on Dunks face.

He woke up scared taking deep breaths and looking around trying to find out what was going on. He was in a lot of pain, his shoulder was bleeding heavily, where the bullet went in and out of.

"What's the code to the safe "Supreme said as he poked Dunk in the chest with the silencer that was connected to the gun. Dunk closed his eyes trying to wake himself up from the nightmare he was in, but when he opened his eyes three masked men were still standing over him.

"let's dead this nigga and carry the safe out" Supreme said." mmmhhm, mhhhmmm, mhhmm" Dunk mumbled "let's see what he has to say." Scoop pulled the tape from off Dunks mouth" this your last chance to save your life. What's the code to the safe?" "If I tell you, you still going to kill me." Supreme fired a shot that missed his head by a quarter of an inch.

"Okay, okay. 79823, fuck! please call the ambulance man, I'm going to bleed to death."

Scoop went to the closet and push the code into the safe and it popped open. Four large stacks of money sat on top of the shelf in the safe with rubber bands on the on them. At the bottom of the safe there were 2 kilos of cocaine. "was it the right code?" Supreme Yelled toward the closet. "Yeah, that's it!" He said.

Supreme kept the pistol aimed at Dunk while Justice went to the closet. "How much was in there? Oh shit... how much you think that is?" "I'm not sure, but it looks like enough to split 3 ways." Said Scoop. He grabbed a brown Gucci backpack and swept all the cash into the bag and tossed the two kilos on top of the money.

"We got what we came for let's get up out of here," Justice said. They both walked back into the room "everything good?" Supreme asked "yeah let's bounce" Justice replied. All three of them began to walk out the room, then Supreme stopped turned around and squeezed the trigger 2 times sending to hollow points into Dunk chest and walked out the room.

Scoop and Katrina got into the front seats, and Justice and Supreme got into the back of the Jeep Cherokee. Scoop tossed the backpack to the back with his boys, started the vehicle and pulled off as the garage door closed.

Supreme and unzipped the backpack, "family, we on like shit now. Oh shit, all this bread was in the safe?" he was excited, and was ready to break down the bread. "Look, I need you to drop me off at the club, so I have an alibi, just in case" Katrina said. "I got you baby" "no, I got you she said.

They pulled up to Scoops car and they all ditched the stolen Jeep Cherokee. They took off their masks as they drove toward the club. Scoop pulled into the parking lot, gave Katrina a kiss and let her out the car. When she walked into the club they pulled off.

6

Scoop check the time, his watch Red 11:11 p.m. he counted the last stack of money. Between 4 people, they all received twenty-seven thousand each. Scoop thought it was only right to give Katrina an equal cut of the money. If it wasn't for her they would still be broke, starting from the bottom.

Katrina proved herself over and over to all three of them. Whenever Scoop and the boys needed anything she came through for them. Scoop found his feelings getting stronger for her as every thought passed through his mind.

"Supreme, justice, pick a stack. They are all the same, twenty-seven thousand, And the 4th stack is for Katrina. I know she said she ain't want nothing but it's only right to give her something." Scoop said. "I aint fucked up About it. I'm grateful" said Justice.

"me too. And we still going to make some bread from the work we got. You know we should celebrate" Supreme said. "oh yeah! What you got in mind?" "Let's go to Katrina's club and throw a couple dollars on her and a couple of fine freaks." "shit, I'm with that" Justice said. "yeah we can do that" Scoop said.

Supreme counted out two Grand and stashed the rest. Justice took two thousand, hid the rest, changed his jeans and shoes and was ready to go. Scoop took two Thousand of Katrina's money and two Grand from his, pulled up the old wooden floor and dropped the cash next to two of his prized possessions. His first pistol, a .22 Cal revolver he caught his first body with, and a picture of his mom and him before she got hooked on Heroin.

She glanced at the picture and he had a flashback of the defining moment that let him to choose the route he was on right now. It was the winter of 02 and he was 12. The power was off, nothing in the refrigerator, and his mom was laid out next to the fireplace unconscious with the needle still in her arm as the fire burned in the winter evening.

For some reason she could always find a way to get high but couldn't come up with any food. He lacked everything, clothes, shoes, jackets, gloves. He didn't have a choice, or a fair shot at life. He felt he was dealt into the Fire. A card game of poker with only three cards, and zero drawls, and no community board.

He pulled out of his mom's arm, and open the cabinet to the lampstand, and there was a. 22 caliber revolver fully loaded. Scoop set the needle down and picked up the gun rolling it back and forth between both hands. He pushed the cabinet closed, stood up and squeeze the gun between his hip and his jeans that were too small. He grabbed his beanie and walked out the house and locked the door. It was cold and almost dark. The wind sent a chill down his spine despite all the years he spent in Detroit, he could never get used to the winters in the city. It was the total opposite of California where it stays sunny and warm year-round.

Scoop pulled his sweater down over his waist, put his hands in his pocket and headed toward the liquor store. He stood outside for a few minutes as he ran through his plan again. He was cold, hungry, and desperate. Just as he got ready to walk into the liquor store one of the hood Hustlers came walking out the store was a brown bag, stuffing a nice stack of money into his right pocket.

Instead of walking into the store he held the door open for the guy, he walked toward his Lincoln Town Car. "Excuse me sir" the guy looked up as he placed the key into the door of the car. "I don't mean to bother you, but I'm trying to get home and I've been walking forever, can you please spare me a ride? I live on St. Mary's right down the road." "Alright you Deanna's son? Scoop looked at him crazy "how you know my mom?" "She's a friend."

"Oh!" "hop in youngsta." Scoop got into the passenger seat and sat back into the heated leather seats as they pulled away from the store. "My aunt lives around the corner from our house. Can you drop me off over there? Our power is off." "Yeah, just point me in the direction."

They turned a couple of corners and Scoop stopped him in front of a house that had on the porch lights, but on the opposite side was an abandoned house.

"Thanks" Scoop said as he reached for his waistband and pulled out the gun. Scoop aimed it with both hands as he pushed his back up against the door. "Give me the money" Scoop yelled. "

"You can't be serious" the guy said. he looked at the little gun and said" you know I know your mom" "shut up and give me the money" he said as his hands shook holding the gun. The guy reached into his right pocket, then jump towards Scoop with his free hand "AAHHH, HHH" he yelled as he reached for the gun. Scoop pulled the trigger three times hitting him two times in the head.

His body went limp and fell onto Scoop. He pushed him toward the driver's window and reached into the guy's pocket and pulled the wad of cash out and got out of the car like nothing ever happened.

He walked toward the abandoned house and cut through the backyard, and he ended up in his own backyard. His sweater had blood on it, and so did his jeans. After that he never looked back.

Scoop placed the floorboard back into place never wanting to be that kid again, the one who had nothing, and this was the chance he waited his whole life for. To become someone and never struggle again. A song from the movie 8 Mile ran through his mind and the lyrics went something like this " you only get one shot, so don't miss your chance to blow, opportunity comes once in a lifetime." "I'll make the best out of this chance. I waited my whole life for this." he said to himself.

He changed his clothes and put his .40 Cal on his hip and they headed out the door. They parked in the lot kind of far away from the door, to get themselves together. They walked towards the entrance "don't be so flashy with the money, we don't want to cause a big scene. We want to enjoy ourselves, but remember we were just broke yesterday. We don't want anyone to put suspicions on us." Justice said ""you took the words right out of my mouth" scoop said.

They pay the cover, got searched, and entered the club. Supreme found a table and they all ordered drinks. There was a dark-skinned cutie with a nice ass and a perky set of tits Supreme instantly zoomed in on.

Before he got his drink, he walked up to the stage and waited for her to come bounce that ass in front of him. She came directly in front of him and squatted down and open her legs. Supreme took a good look and reached into his pocket and pulled out a 20 and reach toward her G-string, leaning toward her and whispered into her ear "come holla at me when you get off stage." he slapped her on the ass, and made his way back to the table.

When he got back to his seat his drink was on the table, and Justice was scoping around for a thick yellow bone. He was into the light bright type of females. They all had a different taste in women. Scoop was waiting for Katrina to come out the dressing room. Scoop picked up his glass "to a new beginning." everyone raised their glass then tipped them back.

Katrina came with two chicks and headed over to wear Scoop and his boys were sitting. Katrina introduced her girls to Justice and Supreme as she sat on Scoops lap. "call the waitress over here baby and order a couple bottles" Scoop said.

"What can I do for ya'll?" "Peach Cîroc and five hundred $1 bills." Scoop handed the waitress the money and she hurried off to the bar. The faster she was the bigger tip she might get. When she got back to the table Katrina tipped her $20 from Scoops pocket. She smiled and went on about her business.

Supremes song came on and hyped him up. He had that dark skin beauty in front of him shaking her ass. He started to make it rain as he vibed to the lyrics of the song. There were ones falling over all three ladies, and they were all enjoying the moment.

They got high and drunk. Justice and Supreme

was ready to take them to a room and get their freak on. A group of niggas came into the club just as Scoop was coming out the bathroom. One of the guys saw his ex-sitting on Supremes lap with his hand between her thighs. He instantly became jealous.

He tried to keep his composure as they walked to the bar. Bo ask the bartender "Who those three corn balls over there?" "I'm not sure but they've been spending tonight." "how long Lexi been over there with that dude?" "maybe 2 hours, a little more" the bartender said.

Bo got up from the bar with his drink in his hand and walked over to Scoop's table. "Lexi let me holla at you for a minute" Bo said. Lexi was sitting in Supremes lap, looked up at Bo ignored him, and continue talking to Supreme.

Bo finished his drink, drop the cup and grab Lexie by the hair. "I said come here bitch." she fell backwards as Bo tried to drag her over by the bar. Supreme got up from his seat and punched him in his face and caused him to fall to the ground. Lexie got up, grabbed her purse, and stood behind Supreme.

Bo's boys peeped the scene and rushed over to where he fell. Scoop and Justice jumped from their seats and started throwing punches not giving the others a chance to react.

Katrina took one of the Cîroc bottles and slammed it over one of the guy's head. The bouncers rushed over and broke up the fight. They made Supreme, Scoop, and Justice left first. As they walked to their car Katrina, Lexi, and Diamond came out "Scoop, please don't do anything stupid. Let's all get out of here and go finish our night." "yeah, let's not let them ruin our night" Lexi said.

"Where are we going?" Supreme said Lexi spoke up "we can all go to my place over on 8 Mile and Telegraph." "I'm with that" Justice said as Diamond smiled at him, they all agreed.

Supreme got his pistol from under the seat and put it in his waistband then got in the car with Lexie. They all followed her as they drove off. They were four cars deep, and Scoop was riding by himself.

7

The bouncers finally let Bo and his boys leave. They decided not to call the police since they got everyone to calm down. They left the strip club and got into a black Expedition. "I'm gone burn that nigga when I catch him." Fuckin Lexi, who this bitch thinks she is? "Meez, drive by Lexis spot." Bo said.

Tray was sitting in the back seat of the SUV holding a bag of ice on his head as they left the club. They made a left on 8 mile and headed toward Telegraph. "Look that's the bitch car about to pull off from the gas station." Meez said.

The light turned green and he pulled the truck into the gas station as Lexi pulled away from the pump. Bo spotted Supreme in the passenger seat. "I'm gone kill this nigga" he yelled as he grabbed the

9 mm from the glove box.

"Pull up on the side of her car" Bo jumped to the backseat of the truck and sat behind Meez as they began to pull up on Lexi's car.

Diamond and Justice was in the car behind Lexi and Supreme, Katrina and Scoop followed her. Meez pulled up on the side of Supreme, Bo rolled the back window down and stuck his arm out the window gripping the 9mm and pulled the trigger.

Glass shattered, and bullets hit the car, flying past Supremes head. Lexi made a hard turn and ran over the median. When Justice seen what was happening, he instantly pulled his gun from his hip and leaned out of the window of Diamonds car and emptied his clip at the expedition.

Scoop reached under the seat and grabbed his .40 Cal and pressed down on the gas and came up on the truck firing at the driver and the passengers in the back. After he emptied his clip he hit the brakes and made a U-turn.

Bo ducked as the bullets flew through the truck. Meez got hit twice and the truck swerved and hit the curb and flipped. Bo, Trey, and Pug bodies were thrown around the truck as it flipped like a gymnast.

Lexi was shaken up, Supreme was bleeding from his neck. Justice and Diamond pulled up to Lexi's car and jumped out "are yall okay?" Justice asked. "I'm good Supreme said. He looked over to Lexi "you okay ma?" she shook her head yeah. "We gotta go before the police get here" Justice said.

Katrina pulled up, then Scoop. "Let's go, follow me to my house" Katrina yelled out her window. Supreme got into the driver's seat and Lexi sat in the passenger seat, and they all took off.

A few minutes later police and ambulance were on the scene. The paramedics approached the vehicle as the police taped off the scene. There was blood all over the inside of the smashed expedition. One of the paramedic opened the door and reached in to check for a pulse of the driver. There was no pulse, Meez was dead.

Bo, Trey, and Pug were unconscious, but they were still breathing. Bo had a broken neck. Trey and Pug had a couple of broken bones but weren't seriously injured. They would live, but the medics weren't too sure about Bo, they figured if he did he may never walk again.

After the paramedics got all the bodies out of the vehicle and loaded onto the ambulance, the police began to go through the truck. There were four hand guns, three of which were fully loaded, a bag of marijuana, and a nice amount of cocaine.

The officers found a few spent shell casings and knew that there was more than one car involved. The Sgt on the scene contacted the police headquarters and told them to contact all the hospitals and let them know if anyone comes in the emergency room with a gunshot wound to contact him.

Bo, Trey and Pug were rushed to Cedar Sinai Hospital to be treated for their injuries. They didn't know if Bo was going to make it, but they were going to do their best to keep him alive.

8

A few days went by and Scoop, Justice, and Supreme decided to go talk to Aunt Mary. Scoop tossed the bag that contained a quarter bird to Justice, and they all got into the car and headed over to 12th street. They all were ready to get to the money.

Supreme slid out the back seat of the car smoking a big Philli filled with Kush weed. When they walked into the house Kim was sitting in the kitchen smoking a joint. Scoop, Supreme, and Justice sat around the table joining Kim.

"How you doin Kim?" said Justice. "I'm fine" "I aint ask how you look, I know you fine, I asked how you doin?" Kim laughed.

"Aunt Mary can I talk to you in the living room" Scoop said. "Yeah, sure" they both went and had a seat on the couch. "I got this work, and we need a trap spot in a decent area. A place where we won't be competing, or on someone's turf,"

"I got this couple that stays on the other side of Hutchins, over the bridge. They always try to get me to come serve out their spot. I know they won't mind if yall set up over there, but they gone want at least a fifty piece a day if you can spare that." Mary said. "I think we can handle that. Why don't you call them and see if we can get it Poppin today, like right now?" Scoop said.

Aunt Mary set everything up and they all headed over to Gina and Coops house. When they got over there they looked around the area, and it was a decent neighborhood, but there were smokers lingering all over looking for a come up, or their next hit.

It looked good to Justice, he knew they would set up shop over there. He was the only one who really had experience selling dope. His dad and older brother had a couple of trap spots he would be in, helping push the dope. Until the DEA hit one of the spots his dad and brother was pushing out of while he was at school.

Justices dad and brother went to the FEDS and left him on the Detroit streets all alone. He had a couple of aunts, but they had plenty of their own kids, and once his dad was gone, everything, and everyone changed how they treated him. He couldn't get a hot meal from anyone, so he found himself roaming the streets. Justice didn't want to be anywhere that he wasn't welcome, so he started nickel and diming on his own.

Justice, Scoop, Supreme and Mary walked into Gina's house and was introduced, then went straight to the kitchen. It was already set up for them to hustle, but they had to cook up the soft, and make it hard.

Justice whipped up the nine ounces and turned it into a little more than eighteen ounces. He put the extra on a napkin and gave it to Gina. She loaded her pipe and took a hit and was instantly high. She passed the pipe to Coop. He took a big hit and tried to hold the smoke as long as he could but started to cough. His eyes got buck and his dick got hard. "Gina bring that napkin to the bathroom. Make yall self at home." Coop said.

Gina and Coop went to the bathroom and locked the door. Justice weighed up sixty-three grams and gave it to Mary. Scoop said "two and a quarter, three grand, and I'll pick up the money in four days." She kissed Scoop on the cheek, "I'll see yall then, be safe and call me if you need me" Mary said.

She made her way back to her spot, and when she got into the house she went to her stash and pulled out her crack pipe and loaded a piece of the sixty-three grams she just got. She took a hit and thought out loud "this some good shit." Mary got on the phone and spread the word that she had some dope, that A1 yola. Her door started swinging, and the money was stacking.

Coop was in the bathroom with his dick in Gina,

stroking her from the back as she hit the pipe. There was a knock at the bathroom door. Supreme was standing on the other end. "Coop, I need to holla at you ASAP." He said "ok" and kept pumping. He finished up, then buttoned his jeans back.

Gina fixed herself and followed Coop to the kitchen. "Do yall think you can spread the word to some of the people yall know? And we might be able to give a bonus for the shit you help us get rid of." Scoop said.

"Yeah, we can spread the word, as long as it's this shit right here. This shit right here is going to have everyone sprung" Coop said. "Shit, the sooner we get rid of this shit the sooner you and Gina get your bonuses." Justice said. "Take a little bit of what we gave you and share a little with some of the people you know? who got money." Scoop said.

Gina and Coop grabbed their jackets and headed out the door. Everyone around the neighborhood knew Coop, he worked on everyone's cars and fixed things around their house. Gina worked a 9-5 but would smoke crack during her off time, she was what you call a functioning addict.

It didn't take long for Scoop, Supreme, and Justice to get their new trap spot jumping. The smokers were back to back trying to cop some of the shit they were selling, but what they didn't know was that they were stepping on someone else's toes.

9

A few weeks had passed, and everything was running smoothly. The money was flowing, and the hoes was jockin. Supremes ego was at an all-time high, he even went and bought him a new Chevy Tahoe, a Rolex, a piece, and a chain. He was hustling anywhere he could. They still had the trap spot, but his eyes were looking at the bigger picture.

He figured if they had multiple spots they would collect more money, and at a faster pace. Scoop knew it would take all three of them to run the spot they had already, and if they had another spot it would take another team, and that they didn't have. So Supreme would pull up to some of the hood stores, and liquor stores and pump the work out the car in the parking lot.

Justice kept it simple and low key, he bought a

2005 GS 350 Lexus and put some dubs on it and tinted the windows. He really didn't need the spot light, he was cool just collecting his money, on call pussy, weed, and bottles whenever he felt like it. He was fine with the trap spot they had, and the money they were bringing in from it. There was more than enough for all of them.

They all agreed to sell the work rock for rock to maximize the profit. The only person they would wholesale to was Mary. That kept everyone from out of their business, and everyone was fine with that.

"Katrina plugged us with the same guy her brother goes through to cop his work, and the quality is supposed to be pretty good. He got a couple spots on the east side on Mack St, and supposedly he runs shit over there." Scoop told Justice.

"Well when are we supposed to go meet him? Cause we down to the last half of a bird, and if we run out, shit who knows how much money we'll miss. I think we should at least grab a whole one, and see what it does, asap.

"I'm going to have Katrina set it up for tomorrow." "Bet, that" said Justice. "Call and see what's taking Supreme so long he was supposed to be here like an hour ago "Scoop said."

Supreme grabbed his phone from off the dashboard and answered it while shorty kept her head bobbing in his lap. "What up bruh?" Supreme said as he pushed back deep into her throat. "Where you at? You know you supposed to had been here an hour ago?" "I'm around the corner. I'll be there in a few." "Aight son, I'm just making sure everything good" Justice said. "Yeah, I'll be there in a minute" Supreme said and ended the call.

He gripped a hand full of hair and began to fuck her face, just as he got ready to nutt he pushed her head as far as it could go and exploded in her throat. She swallowed every drop like a pro and sucked him dry.

"I got to make a move lil mama, but Imma come pick you up tonight" Supreme said and slid her fifty dollars and let her out in the front of her duplex. He watched as she walked away, ass jiggling in her sweats and her upper body warming her double D's from the Park coat she wore. She looked back over her shoulder, smiled, and closed the door.

When Supreme pulled up to the trap he was bumping Gucci Mane "Trap God." He hopped out the truck and turned it off with his push button. The spot was jumpin. When he walked through the door Scoop was in the kitchens chopping up stones, and Justice was controlling the door.

"You know you supposed to be here with us until seven. You been gone for two hours, it takes all three of us to run this ship properly "Scoop said. There were stacks of small bills on the kitchen counter, "I'm not gone even ask where, or what you were doing, bruh just don't fold on us again." I got yall." he said.

"Mary came by and dropped off that bread and picked up four and a half. She said she gone have the money later today, so if you want to make up for that two hours, you can stop by there and pick up that check from her when we close up shop over here and meet us back at the house." "I can do that." Supreme said.

Gina and Coop walked into the spot, "what's going on yall?" Gina said. "What's up T.T" Justice said. He dropped her two decent stones and she kicked off her boots, went and sat on the couch and stuffed her straight shooter, and went to the moon with Coop sitting next to her.

They sold out the shit they had cooked for the day, earlier than they expected, so they shut down the shop. Scoop left a fifty piece on the table for Gina and Coop. "We gone catch yall in the a.m." Coop shook his head up and down.

Scoop put all the money into a plastic grocery bag and stuffed it in his waist band and put his Glock 40 in his coat pocket. They all strapped up and walked out the house. Justice locked the door behind him, and Scoop slid into the passenger seat of the Lexus, as Justice got into the driver seat.

"Don't forget to stop by auntie house." Scoop said as he rolled the window back up. Supreme got into his truck that was already running and pulled off slowly as Justice pulled out of the driveway.

Justice and Scoop pulled onto the Lodge freeway and headed home, as Supreme went to Mary for a pick up. When he pulled up to her house he called, no answer. He called her cell phone, and it went straight to voicemail. He tried a few more times, still nothing.

Supreme gripped his 40 Cal as he jumped out the truck leaving it running and approached the front door. The lights were off. He knocked on the door and rang the bell. Still no answer. He looked around, and walked back to his truck, sat a few minutes, then pulled off.

Supreme rung Scoops phone "house of mackin, what's crackin?" Scoop said laughing. "Did she say she was gone be here? Cause I called both phones, and I knocked on the door. No answer." "Yeah, she said she was gone be waiting, but she probably made a move. She'll be ready later." "Alright, I'm on my way to the house." "Stop and get a fifty box of swishers. We Coppin some cookie right now" "bet, I'll be there in twenty."

10

Mary was strained up, she made a big sale to one of her fades, that set her up with undercover. The Fein didn't know it, she was just trying to get a nice piece of dope for free, and a few extra dollars.

Now Mary was sitting in the backseat of the non-marked police car with a plain clothes officer, and a regular street looking nigga, that was also an undercover officer.

"So, what's it going to be? You give us the person you got the dope from, or we take you down to the precinct and book you in" the officer said. "You know four and a half ounces of crack is a lot out here. Shit if you don't go FED, you're looking at twenty-five years at the minimum. This is your last chance

Mary."

"I don't think she's going to talk, let's just book her and get back out here. We might be able to catch at least two more before our shift is up." He put the car in drive, and just as he began to pull off Mary began to speak.

"If I show you the place, that should be enough right? I can't give you any names because everyone doesn't know him by the same name. If I give you the name he'll know I told you" she said. "What place? Is it a house they sell the dope out of?" "Yes, but that's all I can do." "That's a start." "No, not a start, that's all I can do, and you have to let me walk with the dope." she said.

The officer in the driver seat began to laugh. "You know that's out of the question" "If I don't have their money, I'm dead like two hours ago. If I don't get their money and they get hit, I'm dead either way. This is the only way I can walk away with my life."

"Wrong, you can be a big girl and go do your time," the street looking officer said. "Shut up Gary. This could be a big hit. If you walk away with the dope, and this house turns up empty, we will find you and you will be booked with more than four and a half ounces. Do we have a deal?" The officer asked Mary.

Mary stomach began to turn, and she began to sweat. She didn't want to do what she was about to do, but she felt she had to lookout for herself. "Yeah, we got a deal." The other officer took the cuffs off Mary and he handed the zip loc bag full of crack back to her.

"So, where's the house?" she directed them to Gina and Coops "It's the third house on the left." They drove by at a normal speed as the officers scanned the area. There were a lot of people walking around the neighborhood despite the cold weather. "If you fuck us over, just know that's your ass" the officer said to Mary. They hit the corner and let her out to walk wherever she had to go. "We'll be in touch."

They drove off as Mary started to walk down the street. "I still don't think we should have let her walk with the dope. That was six grand at the least." "If we catch the guy at the right time we might get ten times that. I'll trade that any day for ten times that." "Yeah, me too, but that was for sure money" he said.

They doubled the block to see the back of Mary walk through the front door of Gina and Coops house. "We'll see what happens, we can always squeeze her if shit goes sour."

Mary walked into Gina's house. "Gina, I need you to give me a ride to my place" "girl, where your car at?" "I was riding with a friend of mine and her car broke down on Grand Blvd., so I walked over here. Don't worry I got fifteen dollars for gas." "Ok girl let me get my jacket."

Mary made it to her house and didn't even bother to go inside. She slid into the driver seat of her car, powered on her phone, and made a few calls. She had several voicemails, but before she could listen to them she had to take care of business.

She made a stopover on Greenfield and Plymouth, where she and I met up with one of the guys she sells ounces to, and dumped off the whole package to him for eight grand. He knew she always had that drop, and it wouldn't take him long to make his money back.

When he got into Mary's car his hood was on. He reached into his pocket and pulled out a stack of one hundred-dollar bills and started counting. His hood fell down a little and she could see his face better.

"Damn Keno, what happened to your face? Are you okay?" "Yeah, I'm good M, just some jack boys rolled through and hopped out on me, and took a little bit from me, but it's good, I got some niggas checkin into it. I'm just trying to keep the hustle going" he said. "Yeah, I know what you mean." Mary said. He gave her the bank roll, and she counted. "You be safe out there." "I got it. Keep your eyes and your ears to the streets for me, why don't cha." "You know I got you" she said.

Mary put the money inside of her inner jacket pocket and pulled off. She made a call to Scoop, "what's up Auntie" "can you meet me at the liquor store on the corner I got that gas money for you, and I'm about to head home." "Yeah, I'll be there in a few minutes."

When Scoop pulled up in his car he rolled the

passenger window down. "Everything good auntie?" "Yeah, had to make a few runs, and my phone died, but everything is good. I'm going to need another pack tomorrow, if you can slide through to my house late tomorrow. I'm driving to Grand Rapids early morning, and I'll be back tomorrow late night." "Just hit my line, and I'll make something happen." Scoop said.

"Be safe out there auntie." Scoop pulled out the parking lot with the money and headed back to the house.

Shit was finally looking up for the three of them, he thought. When he got back to the house Supreme had a blunt and a cup of Hennessey waiting on him. They kicked back and chilled making plays for tomorrow.

11

Scoop woke up to a call from Katrina. She set up the meeting with their new plug. "What's up baby?" She said through the phone. "just getting up, I wish you was right here with me. Ain't nothing like waking up next to you" "don't you mean waking up to some morning head?" "That too, but I love just being with you" he said. "Well, I might have to come and spend the night with you again!" "that's a start" Scoop said. "well at 12 this afternoon we got to meet that guy in Southfield. So, make sure ya'll ready, you don't want to be late." Katrina said.

"How about you come over here and make sure I leave on time" "really? I'll be there in twenty minutes Daddy!" "I'll be waiting!"

Scoop let Katrina in through the side door and they went to his room and did they thang. They laid in bed and talked about a future together. "What do you think about getting a place together?" Scoop said. "Only if you think you are ready to get serious, cause I'm fine with the way we are now. I don't want you to feel obligated, I don't want to mess up what we have." Katrina said.

"Every time I think about us it reminds me of Bonnie and Clyde, and I know you a ridah. I'm going to be all the way 100 with you. Katrina, I love you, and everything about you I feel you were made for me like you were tailored or something." "I love you too Darrell. If you really want to take that step just think about it, and make sure that's what you want, but right now we should be getting ready to go meet with Chuco" she said." Okay, well let me get ready." they both got up and took a shower together and got ready. Scoop slid on some True Religion jeans, a polo shirt, and some Aldo sneakers. He stepped up and grabbed his Cartier frames and looked in the mirror.

"You look like a million dollars Daddy" Katrina said to Scoop. Katrina really did have strong feelings for Scoop. She was doing everything she could to change her man circumstances and make him into a winner. She knew he had what it takes to be the man. Charisma, swag, motivation, and of course drive.

She wanted a real future with him, but before they can plan any further she wanted him to be financially stable, and on his feet. "Thank you, baby," he said, and gave her a kiss.

As they walked out the room Supreme and Justice was smoking a blunt. "We got to meet the plug in an hour, and I'm going to ride with Katrina. Yall should follow us and make sure ya'll strapped. I got the bread, so let's just see who and what kind of people we are dealing with."

Justice passed Katrina the blunt, as Supreme and Justice pulled on their Timberlands and grabbed their guns, then threw on their leather coats, and they all walked out the spot.

Justice road in Supremes Tahoe, and Scoop in Katrina's Charger. They hit Southfield and pulled into the parking lot of a Mexican restaurant. Katrina made the call, and they all exited the two vehicles and entered the restaurant.

Katrina walked in first followed by Scoop, Justice, and Supreme. She looked and spotted Chuco sitting in the back of the restaurant, there were several other Mexicans standing around. Chuco Motioned for Katrina and their crew to join him at the table in the back. Katrina, Scoop, and Justice sat down at the table but Supreme remained standing. Chuco spoke "you can have a seat" he said to Supreme, "I'm good, I'd rather stand." "suit yourself." Chuco said. "Katrina, how's your family doing?" "they're good, same shit you know. Well let me introduce everyone. This is Darrel my man and these are his two brothers Justice and Chauncy." she said.

Daryl reached over and shook Chuco's hand "Scoop if you don't mind calling me that, I'm not real fond of my government name, and my other brother that standing goes by Supreme." Chuco asked "are you a 5 percenter, Supreme?" "I don't label myself under any religion, or Creed but I am a student of knowledge, lessons and life. Why do you ask?"

"It's good for me to know as much as I can about the people I will be doing business with and being a 5 percenter means you live by certain code and ethics. Anyways, Katrina by you bringing them here, to me to do business means you are vouching for them, right?"

"I am" she said "well Scoop, Justice, and Supreme. Let me let you know a few things about how we do business, and I'm expecting to keep this between us at this table." Everyone gave a slight head nod, and Chuco began to talk again. "Once you start doing business with us, you can only buy from us. I can assure you the best product that have ever touched the streets of Detroit. We only deal in quantity, and you will be getting it on wholesale. We deal with a large group down in Mexico, and they like their money on time. Since we never done business before we will be giving you the product on consignment, just to cover both of our asses if you know what I mean." Chuco said, Scoop interrupted him "I don't want to interrupt you but that's not how I do business. Me and my brothers don't like to be in people's pockets. We will pay for everything upfront, and if that's not okay with you, I don't want to waste anymore of your time.

Chuco leaned back in his seat and rubbed his

mustache, "It's something I like about you, but just because you have a good quality wouldn't make me do business with you. Only because this young lady that sits next to you, was I willing to meet you, and because of her only will I let you pay up front. I know what kind of woman she is, and I know if she is with you then you must be able to be trusted. One final thing I must say. If you ever cross us, there is nowhere on this earth that you will be able to hide."

"No worries" Scoop said. Katrina pulled out a plastic grocery bag full of one hundred-dollar bills and handed it to Scoop. "We brought seventy-five grand. We need three of them, and if this is not enough I can bring you the rest within an hour."

Scoop tossed the bag over to Chuco. He unwrapped it, and there were mostly stacked hundreds with rubber bands around them. Chuco whispered into one of his guys ears and they took the money to the back of the restaurant. "Would any of you like anything to go? Say a couple of carne asada burritos?" He snapped his fingers and a Hispanic woman with a nice figure came from behind the counter with several bags and placed them on the table and walked back to the cash register.

Supreme couldn't take his eyes off her. He was amazed at the figure she held. He never seen a Mexican with an ass like that. The big Mexican that sat on the other side of the restaurant gave a head nod, and Chuco pushed the bags of food over to them. "Everything is in the bag and I placed a gift inside for you all. Some info for the road, twenty-eight grand a key or you can get them for twenty-five if you get ten or more." Chuco reached over the table and shook Scoops hand, Justice nodded. He also shook Katrina's hand and gave it a little peck. "Cuidado" Chuco said, and she nodded her head.

Supreme took a few steps toward the table and extended his hand and Chuco stood up and their hands locked. "Pleasure doing business with you." Katrina grabbed the bags and they exited the restaurant. "Meet us back at the house." Scoop said.

12

When they all made it back to the house, Scoop began to pull out the food containers. There were four burritos, rice, beans, and red sauce on the side. There were four extra containers, he placed them on the table and opened them up.

There were four kilos of cocaine, one inside of each box. Supreme picked up one of the bricks and began to unwrap it. It was solid like a big piece of concrete. He chipped off a small piece and tapped his tongue onto it. It went completely numb in a matter of seconds.

"This shit right here is as pure as it gets." Supreme said. "Is this really a gift, or is he trying to put us in debt?" Justice asked Katrina." "Chuco is a man of his word, and if he said it was a gift, then that's what it is. You all have the best connect in the city. It took Chuco ten years after my brother turned eighteen to do any business with him. My brother is now thirty-five years old and he's been doing his thing on the eastside for a long time now. My dad use to deal with Chuco a long time ago, until he got busted trafficking bricks to Ohio. He's serving twenty-five years in the FEDS, he has six years left on his sentence. Chuco has been there for my father the whole time. He is really a good person, but he is a businessman" Katrina said.

Scoops phone rang a few times before he answered. "What's up Coop?" "I was calling to see if yall was opening up today, cause the door been jumpin' but I haven't answered because yall aren't here." "Oh yeah, what is it lookin' like out there?" Scoop said. "You must have forgot it's the first of the months huh?" "No, I aint forget I just had some shit to take care of, but we'll be over there soon" "Ok, I'll be waiting" Coop said.

"Coop said the trap was jumping, but aint nobody over there with no dope, and they are waiting around" Scoop said. "Shit, me and Justice can go over to the spot right now." Supreme said. "We missin' money as we speak."

"Take one of these with ya'll and see how they like that shit. I'll put up the rest, and when we get back later tonight, we can bust down everything." Scoop said.

Justice and Supreme grabbed a food container and placed it back into the plastic bag. They put on their coats and headed out the house. They both hopped into separate vehicles and headed to Coops house.

Scoop walked back to his room, and pulled up the floor board, and dropped the Kilos in the stash spot. He seen the picture of him and his mom again and had a flash back.

Scoop was eight years old, and he was riding in the backseat of his moms 96 Delta. They pulled up to his aunt's house and went inside. He was sent out to the backyard where all the kids were playing. He was dressed nicely in Guess jeans and a Polo shirt. He found his cousin in the group of kids and they gave each other a high five. Michael was a year older than Scoop, and a lot bigger. He could have passed for a twelve or thirteen-year-old.

He had influence over a lot of kids, but it was the opposite when it came to influencing Scoop. "Scoop I got some stuff to show you up in my room." They left all the other kids playing in the backyard and headed into the house. When Scoop and Michael made it to his room, he went into his closet and pulled out an old shoe box. He grabbed a few pictures and handed them to Scoop. "Holy shit! Where did you get these from?" There were about ten pages torn from the playboy magazine, that showed it all.

"I found them in this abandoned house. I know these two girls that let me kiss and feel on their butts, and they said they were going to do the same thing these girls in the pictures are doing. So, they be practicing all the time." "Let's go see if they're outside." Scoop said. They both got up and walked out the room. Michael heard his mother screaming and he ran into her room with Scoop right behind him. Deana was laid out on the floor convulsing and shaking. "Call 911 Michael Now!" She yelled. She rolled Deana on her side, so she wouldn't choke.

Michaels mom stashed the heroin before the ambulance arrived. "Don't say anything Darrell, you don't want them to know she is your mom because CPS might get involved and take you away." She said.

Scoop watched his mother get placed on a stretcher and rolled out of the house and taken to the hospital. He stayed with his aunt and cousin for a week while his mom recovered in the hospital. He was left to fend for himself. He and Michael made things work. This is when his life started to go in a downward spiral.

Katrina interrupted his train of thought. "Are you okay baby?" She said, as he snapped out of his flash back. "Yeah, I'm ok." He placed the floor board back into its place, stood up and kissed Katrina. "Do you want to grab some Coney Island? I aint really feelin' the burritos right now." Katrina said.

"Yeah, I could go for a Corn Beef sandwich and some chili cheese fries." Scoop said. They got into Katrina's car and went to the Coney Island on six mile and Greenfield. Scoop ordered for them both and as he paid, a guy walked in with two other men. He had stiches over his left eye and a tattoo on the right side of his neck that said P. Rock.

Scoop was handed his food through a bullet proof glass window, and as he turned around he had a clear look at the guys face. It was the same person they jacked a few weeks ago. The guy looked at Scoop and was trying to remember where he seen him before. Scoop motioned for Katrina to get up, as he put his hand in his jacket pocket and gripped the berretta 9mm.

They got into the car "Let's go baby," "what's wrong Scoop?" "That was one of the niggas that we took down a few weeks ago." Just as they began to pull out of the parking spot and onto the street the guy ran into the parking lot with his gun out trying to figure out what car they got in, but Katrina's charger had tinted windows. The sun hit the passenger window and he seen a glimpse of Scoop.

He aimed and opened fire at Katrina's car, she smashed on the gas fish tailing as the hemi screamed and sped away through the wet street. A few bullets hit the back of the car, but they were able to get away unharmed.

"I'm sorry baby for you having to go through this." "Don't apologize, shit happens." "I've been meaning to give this to you, but never had the chance to." He reached into the inside of his leather coat pocket and pulled out the twenty-five grand. This is your share from the lick we hit. I know it's an

awkward time, but maybe it will lighten the mood."
He sat a large stack of hundreds in her lap as she
drove. Katrina looked down as she drove and seen
the money, her eyes began to water. She did her best
to control he emotions but felt herself falling in love
more and more.

She didn't think he would be willing to give up
such a large amount of money knowing his
background, and how much of a struggle he went
throughout his life.

She really didn't need the money, but the
gesture opened her heart more to Scoop. "Why are
you giving this to me Scoop?" "Because you deserve
it. If it wasn't for you none of us would be in the
position we are in now. We would still be struggling,
having nothing. I never in my life met a woman like
you, and I never want to lose you. I love you Katrina,
and I have never loved a woman because my heart
wouldn't let me. I thought all women were the same,
and you changed my mind about that." He said.

"I love you too Scoop, and I'll always be here for
you." Katrina said. Scoop sat back and fired up the
blunt that was in his ashtray, trying to calm his
nerves. He passed the blunt to Katrina, and she took
a deep drag on the swisher. "Do you think you can
be with only one woman?" "She asked. "You are the
only woman I've been with in the last ten months,
and all I want is you. So, to answer your question,
yes I can."

They pulled up to Gina and Coops spot. "You

can come trap with me if you like." He said, with a smile on his face. "No daddy, I'm going to bust a few moves, but I'll come spend the night with you." "I'm down." They kissed, and he got out the car and walked into the trap spot as she drove off.

Scoop used the key he got from Gina and walked into the house. "Yo, I thought you said it was jumpin," he said as he closed and locked the door. Coop had on his coat and was standing on the back porch. Justice was still cooking the bird, and Supreme was trapping out the back-burglar bars. They made Coop feel like he was earning his keep, but they really didn't want him to know how much dope they were cooking.

Instead of using the front, all the fades were coming through the ally and up to the back porch while Coop made the hand to hand sales. He knew everyone in the neighborhood and would not sell to an unfamiliar face. "I see yall got it jumpin' from the back." Scoop said. "Yeah, it was Coops idea to make everyone come up the ally and, in the back, so nobody sees all the foot traffic. We figured it was a good idea, so we let Coop orchestrate it. Let him feel like he is earning his keep. And if something happens its going from his hand into theirs. If you know what I mean." Supreme said. Justice finished cooking up the last of the brick. "Man, cooking all that shit got me fucked up. Roll up something to smoke. I need some Kush in my life." Justice said.

He washed his hands in the kitchen sink, as he

looked through the curtain the fiends kept coming. Justice picked up his 9 mm and placed it on his hip. "I think this shit might be better than that other dope we came up on, cause they aint stop comin' since I placed the first ten rocks in Coops hand." Said Supreme. "We already ran through an ounce and a half, and they still coming" Justice said.

Supreme handed Coop twenty dime rocks through the burglar bars and closed the door. "Light that blunt and quit playing." Justice said.

A silver Chrysler 300 pulled up a few houses down from the trap spot. "Where's all the foot traffic if they supposed to be clocking? You don't think that old bitch told them what happened do you?" "I don't think she would if she knows what's best for her. Just chill, we gone lay low here for a minute and see what's going on." "Check it, you think that new Tahoe belongs to Mr. Dope man?" "It's possible," "It still got the dealers tags on it. Whosever it is, is spending some bread on it. If this nigga holding like she said he is, I'm going to buy me one of those. No, better yet a Denali. Yeah, a Denali those are nice. I can get a lot of ass in that." He said.

They sat in the Chrysler until the Sun began to go down. The driver began to fall asleep. "Look, look, somebody coming out. He sat up in his seat. Three black males came out and locked the door. Scoop got into Supremes Tahoe, and Justice pulled off in his Lexus with Supreme tailing him.

"Are we going to follow them?" "Yeah, just chill.

You are acting like you aint never done this before," They waited for them to hit the corner before they started the car. He sped up trying to catch up but keeping a good distance behind them.

Inside the Tahoe Supreme pulled a Philly out the ashtray and sparked it. "Oh, this how you smoking on your own huh?" Scoop said and laughed as Supreme passed the blunt to him. He took a hit and sat back in his seat, "I gotta tell yall what happened today. I waited until we closed the shop, cause I aint want it to affect our hustle."

"What is it?" Supreme said urging him to answer the question faster than he was able. "That nigga we jacked over on Plymouth came into Coney Island while me and Katrina was picking up our food. I noticed him but played it cool and motioned for Katrina to follow me outside. We got into the car and as we pulled off he ran outside. I guess he noticed my face. He came off the hip and started shooting at the car and hit it a few times."

"What? You know we gotta go handle that. We can't let that nigga walk around and speak up on us. And that nigga shot up my sister car. You know I aint having that." "The only reason I aint put the nigga down right there, cause I aint want to put her through anymore shit. If I Knew he was gone shoot at us, I would of dead that nigga right there. And he had two of his niggas with him. Let's go slide over through their hood and see if we can spot him." "Nah, let's just wait. They probably expecting us to come through there."

Supremes phone rang "Say ask Scoop if he wants to stop at the sports bar and have a few drinks" Justice said. "Nah we gone slide to the spot, we already got a couple of bottles in the freezer. Let's all go lay low, and we still gotta break down that other shit." "Alright." Justice said and pressed the end button on his cell.

"You peep that car following us? He been behind us for a minute now." Scoop said. He got on the phone "Justice take that shit to the house, we gone be there in a minute. We got somebody tailing us. I'm about to take care of it, park in the back and leave space for us.

Scoop pulled the Glock off his hip, "Slow down a little bit," Supreme put his blinker on and made it seem like he was going to turn. Scoop hung out the window and unleashed his whole clip at the Chrysler, they hit the brakes and made a hard turn. Supreme sped off and hit a few corners and made it to the house. Scoop jumped out and watched for any approaching cars as Supreme put the truck into the garage in the back.

They went into the house, and Supreme was hype. "You should have seen it, this nigga hung out the truck like he was Desperado and lit they shit up. "That boy Scoop back." He said as he popped open a bottle of Remy V.S.O.P.

"I aint ever went nowhere. I do what you should do and think before I act. I refuse to let anyone slide up on me anymore. If you notice, I've been shot at twice in the last month. I rather be the one shootin'. I think I'll live longer that way." Scoop said as he poured himself a cup of Remy.

"I told you we were too close. What the fuck was you thinking? You could have got us killed." "We alright, you aint get hit, did you?" We know what we are dealing with now. When we get the drop on them we just gone have to go in guns blazing." "I don't know." "Don't say you pussying out on me now. This could be the one we been searching for. Tell me how many people gone do what they just did if they aint have a large amount of money or dope on them?" "I'm just saying, we gotta be smarter than that. We might need another person or two to help us." "And get a cut of my share? Fuck no, we got this." "Whatever you say." "I'll think of something. I always do!"

13

Mary didn't want any part of whatever was about to unfold. She was taking it hard on herself. "I should have kept my mouth shut. I hope they are ok, she said to herself. She was on the seventy-five-freeway headed down to Atlanta, she packed up all her valuables and left the rest. She was looking for a fresh start with the money she had saved up. Mary never thought she would move away from Detroit, but she felt she had no other choice.

She knew if her nephews found out what she did, they wouldn't have any mercy on her. She knew they were cutthroat when it came to snitching. Number one rule keep your mouth shut.

Atlanta was a nice place to start but figured she would end up in Houston. She always heard good things about Texas, and Houston was on her mind. She turned up the radio, and lit a joint, then jammed out to Bootsy Collins "I rather be with you, yeah! Yeah, I rather be with you. Yeah. I wanna hold you in my arms 'til the break of dawn."

She sang along as she tried to keep her mind off what might happen to the three people that always showed her love and was willing to help her with whatever. They would have even killed for her, but she chose to throw them under the bus. She couldn't stand to watch them get ran over, so she took off.

Back in Detroit Katrina was pulling off the lot in a brand-new Dodge Challenger on 22s, it was Detroit Lion blue, with dark tint and a grey racing strip. She pulled up to the house where Justice, Supreme and Scoop was. She called Scoops phone "baby, ya'll come outside" "What? why? Come in the house" he said. "Come outside, I want yall to meet somebody." "Who the hell you brought over here?" He said with an attitude, as he paused the PS4 and looked out the window.

"Who is it?" Supreme said as he looked out the window next to Scoop." I don't know but that Challenger clean." Scoop said. "I'll be out in a sec. Let me grab my jacket." He hung the phone up and threw on his leather Pelle Pelle coat. Justice and Supreme stepped out onto the porch with him. Katrina jumped out the driver seat and screamed "surprise!" And ran up the stairs and gave him a hug and a kiss. She placed the keys in his hand as Justice and Supreme stood back in Shock.

Scoop was stuck and didn't know what to say.

Katrina grabbed him by the hand and pulled him down the steps. "Get in, let me see how you look in it." She said. Supreme and Justice walked down off the porch to get a better look at it. Scoop got into the driver's seat and looked around. It was fully equipped, sunroof, CD player, and an interior that was navy blue suede. "Hit the gas." She said. He pushed down and the engine roared, the car moved from side to side. Supreme jumped "Oh, my nigga on." This bitch clean, and it's the Super Bee edition." Scoop stood up out the car and grabbed Katrina and said it loud and clear in front of his boys. "I love you," and gave her a kiss. "Let's go for a ride" he said. She ran around to the passenger side and got in. Scoop pulled the car door closed, he rolled the window down, "yall get dressed, we are going out tonight."

"Shit you aint said nothing but a word." Supreme said. He put the car in reverse and pulled out the driveway. When he got to the street Katrina turned up the music and the bass rattled the windows on the house. "Damn." Justice said.

Scoop hit the gas and burned out the whole block. "Bro got to keep her, he should just go ahead and marry her. I wonder if she got two sisters she aint tell us about." Justice said. "Come on nigga, let's go roll up some weed and get ready to go stunt in the club. What you should do is trade in that Lexus and come new. You the only one who aint fresh off the lot." Supreme said. "Yeah, but my shit cashed out, and I'm stacking'." Justice said, even though he was contemplating something new.

Scoop and Katrina was flipping through the whole westside. They were very much in love with each other and loving each other's company. "What made you get this car for me?" "I was tired of seeing you in that bucket." She laughed. "To be real, when I had seen it, I instantly thought of you. It fits you and your personality, and you deserve it." "Well, just to let you know I love it." "I know, I could tell by the look in your eyes. I want you to meet my brother if you're ok with that?"

"I was starting to think I wasn't ever going to meet any of your family. When?" "Right now, actually. He's at my place." "Okay," he said. They pulled up into Katrina's driveway behind a black Audi A8 that sat on 24inch Forgiato rims. The license plate read DKING. They got out the car and walked through the front door. Katrina's brother was on the couch watching Friday and smoking a big philly blunt of some California Kush.

"Brother." Katrina said, he turned his head and seen his sister. "I want you to meet Darrell, a.k.a Scoop, my man. Scoop this is my brother Dion aka D. King." "So, this Mr. Special you've been talking about? Huh." He reached out to shake Scoops hand. Dion stood six five and weighed two hundred and thirty pounds. "You smoke?" He asked Scoop, "Yeah," Dion passed him the philly. "Have a seat. Excuse us for a minute Trina, I wanna talk to Scoop in private." "What?" "This is my house!" "I know sis, please just give us a few minutes." "Don't be on no B.S Dion." Katrina walked up the stairs and went to change clothes. She was going with Scoop, Justice, and Supreme even if he didn't invite her. Which she was sure he did.

"I know I don't know you, but Trina tells me a lot about you. I've been taking care and looking out for my sister for the past nineteen years, since I was sixteen. My mom left us at a young age, and my pops got a twenty-five-year FED sentence when I was eighteen. He got locked up in the county when I was sixteen. We had no family, just each other. I had to do a lot to take care of her, made sure she finished school, and not want for anything. I was basically her father, brother, and best friend. We've been through a lot, and I don't want my little sister to get hurt." DK said.

"Your story kind of sounds like mine, but my mom was a heroin addict, and she left me on my thirteenth birthday, and never came back. I made a way out of no way, and here I am today, in the position I'm in now because of your sister. She helped me make the right moves, and I can see now, she learned from you. I gotta be honest with you, but I don't want to offend you." Scoop said.

"By all means speak your mind." "I love your sister, not only love her, but I'm in love with her." They both sat there quite for a minute. "I wouldn't expect anything less. All I have to say is take care of her and do her right, and if you ever need anything or anyone to talk to just call me." DK said, he reached across the table and shook Scoops hand.

Katrina walked into the living room wearing a silk navy blue Gucci blouse, seven Jeans that looked painted on, and to top it off she had on some knee-high Jimmy Choo's. "How do I look?" Katrina asked while spinning in a circle.

"You look like the black queen you are. Or should I say my queen." "I like the second one better." she said. "You look good lil' sis." "Thank You. We gone kill 'em tonight." "Maybe you want to meet up with us tonight DK. We slidin through KOD'S." "Yeah, I might slide through there and show yall some love." "I'll see you later brother." "Take care of her Scoop." DK said. He nodded his head as they walked out the door.

They stopped at Northland Mall and grabbed Scoop a new True Religion fit and some Jordan 6's. He put on his new clothes in the dressing room and came out looking clean. Scoop called Justice, "Are yall ready? Cause I'm ready for the takeover." "Yeah, we about to walk out the door now."

"Good 'cuz we pulling up right now." Supreme and Justice got in separate vehicles just in case they pulled a shorty from the club, they would be able to do their own thang with no issues.

Everyone was strapped as usual. They pulled up three cars deep, and parked in VIP at the front of the club. The three of them came out of pocket and paid for a VIP table and two bottles.

Everyone was enjoying themselves. Justice was in his own zone, throwing dollar bills over a thick chocolate chick. Supreme was standing up feeling himself, he had a stack of ones throwing them in the air every time a dark-skinned shorty walked by. A few redbones tried their luck, and he didn't want to throw anything or pay for any dances. But a fine yellow bone approached him, she was about 5'3, long hair and a nice ass.

"How are you doing?" she asked. "I'm Gucci." Supreme said. "Hi Gucci, I'm Dior" Supreme started laughing. "What's funny?" "I was saying I'm Gucci, as in I'm doing ok." "Oh! Well what's your name?" "Supreme." "Are you like a fiver percenter or something?" "What you know about any of that?" he said. "Don't let my looks fool you, there's brains behind this beauty." "Oh really?" "Yes, really. And if you took some time to get to know me you would find out for yourself." "Well, not to be rude but I'm not really in to light skin chicks." "There you go judging by looks again. Just because I'm bright skinned doesn't mean that I'm not the blackest woman you will ever meet." Supreme laughed, "well let's have a seat so I can pick your brain."

They both took a seat at the far end of the bench and continued their conversation. Not long after Supreme and Dior sat down, a group of fifty people walked through the door, every one of them wearing black shirts with MSG on them, and one of them wearing a white T that said D KING.

The DJ was on the mic "oh shit yall, its D KING and the whole MSG. The true ballers just entered the building. So, all you niggas that aint tippin' it's time to go cause this real money here." Katrina and Scoop sat back smiling "He made one hell of an entrance. I didn't expect that." Scoop said. "Yeah, he always has to be the center of attention."

Dior asked, "Do you know who that is?" "No, why? Would you like to go over there?" "No, it just looks like they are all coming this way."

DK bought out the rest of VIP for all his niggas, there was bottles and bitches galore. He walked over to where Katrina and Scoop were sitting. Katrina got up and gave him a hug. "Do you always have to steal the show?" she asked. Scoop stood up and they shook hands.

"I thought you didn't know him" Dior said. "I don't but give me a second." Supreme and Justice stood to the side of Scoop as he spoke to DK. "Well I'd like to introduce you to my brothers. This is Justice, and Supreme."

They all shook hands, "This is Katrina's brother." "So, you run MSG? You the one they call King of da Eastside!" "Nice to meet you" DK said.

Dior sat at the end of the bench watching everything unfold. She was just happy to be in the presence of some real players. She was tired of all the broke, bum, nothing going for themselves niggas. The ones that come in the club buy one beer and just watch the stage.

DK sent one of his boys to go tip the DJ, and to give a few shout outs. A few minutes later Katrina, Scoop, Supreme and Justices name was blasting through the speakers. "This goes out to the real playas and ballers in here. Shout out MSG, the whole east side, and to the three of the biggest niggas of the Westside, six mile in this bitch!" The DJ said.

They all looked over to DK and he held a bottle of Remy X.O up in the air and saluted all three of them. Supreme went and sat back with Dior, leaned into the cushion, and rolled a philly of some Kush he had. "You can help yourself to a drink if you fuck with Cîroc," he said. She poured a cup. "Do you smoke?" "Like a chimney." She said. "I like how you are so laid back," she said. "Most niggas be so aggressive, trying to touch, and feel. They be in a rush trying to get my number and trying to take me home."

Supreme looked at her from the corner of his eye, as he finished rolling the blunt. "Well, I told you that I wasn't really into light skinned chicks. Who said I'm not aggressive?" Dior got up from the couch and straddled Supreme and looked in his eyes. He exhaled the smoke and blew it into her face, she took the blunt and hit it. She took the smoke that was in her mouth and put her lips on Supremes and blew the smoke into his mouth. He inhaled and gave her a light kiss. He looked deep into her eyes, trying to discern if she was being real or just looking for a ticket.

Justice came over and interrupted them, "say bruh, come with me to the bathroom." Supreme looked up at Justice and back at Dior. "Come on nigga, I got to piss. You takin your precious ass time, and you don't even like yella bones!" Justice said. Supreme whispered in Dior's ear "I'll be back, if you're here cool, if you get pulled by another nigga, your choice." He said as he lifted her off him. She gave him kind of a rude look and sat down on the couch. He reached for the blunt out of Dior's hand, and walked toward the restroom with Justice. There was a group of niggas sitting at the bar watching the stage as they sipped their drinks. Justice and Supreme walked in front of the stage to get to the restroom.

"Say that's two of the niggas that jumped out on me over in the hood." "So, what you want to do? All the straps are in the car."

Justice pissed in the urinal, as Supreme watched his back. He washed his hands and they made their way back across the club. Supreme could see Dior still sitting on the couch in the VIP area and laughed to himself. "What's wrong with you bro?" "What you mean?" "When did you start liking yella bones? Justice asked. "I don't know. I don't, it's just something about this chick." Supreme said as they were bumped into by two guys and surrounded by eight more. Dior caught the whole play before it even went down and ran over to Katrina and Scoop.

"Look them niggas got Supreme and your other boy surrounded."

Scoop jumped up and Katrina followed. He rushed over through the crowd and got to his brothers. DK seen Katrina and Scoop rushing over to a group of niggas and he instantly knew something was wrong. He gave his signal and walked through the club with all fifty of his niggas close behind him.

"What's the problem?" Scoop said as he pushed his way into the circle where Supreme and Justice stood. "Who you supposed to be superman?" One of the niggas in the crowd said. "Nah that's the driver." "Let's three for one these niggas then." Scoop looked at the nigga and instantly got hot. It was the nigga they robbed a few months ago. The same nigga that shot at Katrina's car about a week ago. What they didn't notice was the whole MSG niggas surrounding them. DK pushed the first nigga he encountered, and he flew to the ground.

"What's the problem over here?" Dk asked. All the niggas looked around and seen that they were outnumbered, and nobody said anything. "So, all yall bitches mimes now?" Then Keno spoke "D King, this aint got nothing to do with you," "I think it does Keno, so tell me what the problem is?" "These three niggas robbed me on the corner when I was trappin and took everything I had, they even slapped me over the head with a pistol." Keno said. He looked over at Scoop and seen the anger on his face. Keno was trying to plead his way out of trouble that he placed himself in.

"Well you should be on top of your game then. How much did they take from you?" DK said as he reached into his Robin jeans pulling out an extremely large stack of hundreds. Twenty-five hundred including my dope." "You are crying over pocket change. You lucky you walked away with your life." DK counted out twenty-five hundred and folded it up and tossed it in his face. "Now if you don't want any problems you will pick up the money and leave. Just so you know these are my lil' brothers." Scoop stepped up and said "don't give that bitch shit, he's the reason why there's bullet holes in Katrina's Charger."

DK looked back at Katrina, and she looked down. He looked back at Keno. "You shot up the car while my little sister was in it?" DK said. Keno started to get scared for the first time.

The DJ came on the mic "can't we all just get along. Let's throw some money, and sip some drank." DK turned and said something into the ear of one of his boys and he walked out of the group. About fifteen of his boys exited the club a few minutes later they came back in.

"If you want to live another day you are going to take your boys here and leave right now if you know what's good for you." DK said. Keno reached down to pick up the money but DK's foot stepped on it.

"You forfeited the money, after you left holes in my sisters car. I think you should pay for that. So, let's call it even. Now get the fuck up out of here before I feel like your testing my patience." Keno turned around and DK's boys made an exit for them, and Keno and his boys walked out of the club.

"I know we just aint about to let them handle us like that?" One of Kenos shooters said. "It's ten of us, and fifty plus of them, what the fuck else we supposed to do?" Keno said.

"Let's wait until they leave the club and wet they ass up" he said. "Don't be stupid. Let's get the fuck up out of here before we not get another chance." They all loaded into two Suburban's and pulled out the parking lot of the club.

A black Nissan Maximum pulled out the other side of the parking lot with three people in the car. They all had on black beanies. The backseat passenger was holding an AK-47 in both of his hand waiting for his opportunity to make a name for himself. The Nissan Maximum pulled next to the first Suburban and rode alongside of it for a few seconds. "Don't shoot yet, wait for a red light, then we gone take flight." The front passenger said.

The light flashed from yellow, to red. Before the Maxima could come to a complete stop, the person in the backseat threw the car door open and jumped out squeezing the trigger with every step he took toward the two trucks.

He hit both drivers and sprayed each truck like he was painting them with bullets. When the gun stopped firing he got back into the car and they made a left turn at the light and drove off like nothing happened, leaving the truck looking like swiss cheese.

The driver made a call, he could still hear music playing in the background "It's done," "Good, get rid of the car and the gun, and go chill in the hood until we get there." "Alright" the driver said and hung up the phone.

DK was talking to Scoop and Katrina "Yall make sure you call me if you need anything. And Scoop I aint gone say this again. Take care of my sister. Yall get up out of here, we bout to smash too." DK said he left the twenty-five hundred dollars that he threw in Kenos face as a tip for the waitress, and they all walked toward the exit. "A shout out to D King and the whole MSG for coming and showing us some love tonight." The DJ said. They all got in their whips and made their way to the house.

14

Monday came around and they were back trapping at Coupe spot. Gina was at work but was just about to get off. It was 5:30 p.m. when a black Impala pulled up in front of the spot and two men got out and started walking towards the door.

The trio was sitting in the dining room around the table talking as Coop was outback doing his thing, hand-to-hand, and directing foot traffic. All three of their guns were sitting on the table next to a few stacks of fives tens and twenties.

The two men walked up the steps and tried to peek through the window. No one was visible. "I know they're in there, the same Lexus is right there." "Yeah, or they made a move and rode in the truck together." "well this might be a good time to go in. I know they got something in there, and since we aint seen nobody at the door all day, they probably changed their hours."

The taller man put his ear to the door and heard nothing. "Stand to the side while I kick this bitch open." they both pulled their weapons off they're hip, he took a step back and kicked next to the deadbolt. it budged a little.

"What the f*** was that?" Supreme said as he grabbed his gun." Get the money and the dope Justice." who grabbed his gun and went into the kitchen and peeked around to the front door.

He kicked the door again and it flew in, "let's go, sweep left, I'll go right." When they got through the threshold they pushed the door back up slowly, but it wouldn't close.

Scoop peeked around the corner in scene two men, both black wearing leather jackets with their guns out. "One more step, and I'm going to blow his head off his shoulders" he thought to himself. Scoop looked back to see Justice, the money and his guns slipped out the back door. "What the fuck this nigga think he doing?"

Scoop hid around the corner to see them splitting up "now" he said to himself. He stepped from behind the wall and began to unload his 40 Cal, boom! Boom! Boom! Bop!! Bop!! the guys started squeezing his Ruger without aiming. He tried to dive behind the couch, but before he could turn he was hit by one of Scoops bullets. "AAhhhhhh, I'm hit!" he yelled. His partner tried to take cover, but Supreme came out of nowhere and pulled the trigger. The bullet went right through the back of the guy's head. Supreme kick the gun out his hand.

The other guy was still shooting trying to keep Scoop back, he didn't hear anything from his partner. He was hoping he was making some ground on sneaking up behind Scoop.

"I told him we should have come with two more people," he whined to himself as he pushed in another clip and kept firing. "Hurry the fuck up and take this guy out: he thought.

Justice came and crept up the steps and push the door open slowly with his 9 mm in his hand, he crept around to see one of the guys laying on the ground firing over the couch toward the kitchen.

Justice took aim and unloaded his clip at the guy on the floor hitting him about 9 out of 10 times. He didn't move or fire his weapon anymore. "Let's go" Justice yelled. Scoop and Supreme came running through the house and they all left and jumped in the Lexus and pulled off. They left Scoop with the last work and money he made from the hand-to-hand fade he was making in the back.

Justice as made sure to tell Coop to keep his mouth closed and call Gina and ya'll get Somewhere. "you know what happens to snitches right?" He's so cool.

"What the fuck was all that about?" I just asked. "I think somebody was trying to Jack us." "How many of them were there?" "I only seen two." "yeah, and I blew the other niggas brains out." Supreme said confidently.

"What the fuck we gone do now? We don't got nowhere to sell this shit, and we got to worry about these two bodies. What if that Nigga run his mouth?" "I can take care of him and Gina." "and what will Mary think?" Justice said. "I'm about to call her" Scoop said as he pulled his cell out and held the number four down.

"I'm sorry this number has been disconnected," he tried it again, and the same thing happened.

"What's up?" "Her number is disconnected." "That aint like her." "Fuck!" Scoop yelled. "We got to get rid of these guns, and this car." "I aint getting rid of my car" Justice said in a serious tone. "Do something with this bitch, cause I aint going to prison because you don't want to get rid of it. Sell it, paint it, or trash it. I don't give a fuck what you do but it bet not be this same color and you better not drive it no more" Supreme said.

Justice gave Scoop the dope and the money and pulled off as they walked into the house. "Aint nobody asks this nigga to get rid of his truck when Scoop was hanging out the window shootin' at people."

He felt attached to the Lexus. It was his first car, he couldn't even remember when his mother had a car. They were always walking or riding the city bus.

He pulled up at the 24-hour paint and body shop in East Warren and paid them to Prime and paint it. They told him 2 weeks, so he called a cab and headed back to the house. By the time he got back Supreme and Scoop was throwing all their clothes in duffle bags.

"What's going on?" Scoop answering him, "that shit made the news, and these two niggas that kicked the door in was DPD officers, and one of them is still alive. Get your shit, we got to get out of town." "and go where?" "I got a cousin out on the West Coast" Scoop said. "And how we going to get there? We going to get on the bus? Or what?" "Justice get your shit, we gone tonight!"

Scoop was wrapping the bricks they had got a few days ago, he put some clothes in separate duffle bag. Supreme was the first one ready he took his things to the back where his Tahoe sat next to the Challenger and put them in a backseat.

"Let's go, we got to get the fuck out of here." Supreme said. "look Supreme we going to take the truck, and the Challenger but we going to put the dope in the truck. One person in the truck at a time. If the police Get behind you for any reason Don't Panic, we going to fly past speeding to get his attention, just keep driving no matter what. We'll catch back up and keep your phone on the charger." Scoop made clear. If we drive straight through it will take 24 hours to get to Vegas. Once we make it out of Nebraska we should be okay."

Justice threw his bags in the trunk of the Challenger with Scoops duffle bags. They loaded up and jumped onto the 96-freeway heading towards

Chicago.

Supreme was leading the way, he was following the GPS map on his phone, he had four and a half bricks, and about twelve hundred in his pocket. The rest of the money was in the car with Scoop. A few hours later they were entering Iowa. They stopped just shy of Des Moines and gassed up," you want to switch now Scoop asked Supreme? "Nah I'm good. let's just get to where we are going," "just let me know when you want to switch" Scoop said.

They got back on the road, and they were about 20 hours from Las Vegas. Justice as pulled out a blunt and lit it, "what the fuck do you think you doing?" Scoop said as he snatched the blunt out his mouth and threw it out the window. "We already riding dirty, we don't need any extra reasons to get stopped and taken in."

Justice didn't say shit, he just sat back in his seat and looked out the window. He started to drift off, Justice had a lot of thoughts going through his mind, but decided to relax, and let go of all the worry. He was knocked out before he knew it.

15

Justice woke up to sirens and police lights. "What happened? Where we at?" "We just crossed the state line into Colorado. They seemed like they were going to pull Supreme over So I started going about 15 miles over the speed limit. Put your seatbelt on and be cool."

Supreme looked in his rear-view mirror and seen Scoop pulling to the side of the highway and kept driving.

The officer was a tall white redneck. He walked up to the passenger side window and waited for the window to roll down. "How you fellas doing?" He asked.

"We doin alright, how about you sir?"

"Just Working young man. This a pretty nice ride you got here."

"Thank You."

"Do you know why I pulled you over?"

"Yes sir, I was speeding."

"Yeah, and your car looked good doing it. Where you guys headed?"

"Las Vegas! We're meeting my girlfriend out there, and a few of her friends. I'm getting married tomorrow."

"Let me get your license and registration."

Scoop pulled his driver's license and registration, along with his insurance from his visor and handed it to the officer. He looked at the picture and looked back at Scoop. "You fellas from Detroit?" He asked.

"Yes, sir we are."

"Well I be God dang. I'm from Southfield. How about those Lions?" He asked them.

"Had a good season, just need a running back. Stafford a hell of a quarterback but can't do it by himself. We might make it to the Superbowl next year if we pick up a good back!" Scoop said.

The officer was pleased to share a little back and forth about his team with fellow Lions fans and hometown natives.

"You guys slow down out here. The seventy freeway aint no joke, especially once you get into those Rocky Mountains", He handed Scoop all his paperwork back "nice paint job. Go lions" he yelled, as he walked back to his highway patrol car.

"Call Supreme and see how far he is." Justice pulled his phone out his hoodie and rang Supremes phone.

"Yall good?" he said.

"Yeah, we straight,"

"You'll never believe what happened."

"What?"

"I'll tell you in a minute, where you at?"

"I'm passing exit 121,"

"Alright" Scoop said, "slow down a lil bit, we gone catch up we passin exit 105. Go seventy and we should catch up to you in about thirty minutes."

"Alright, bet."

"Be careful" he said.

"Awe look at you being all worried about us. We love you too bruh."

"Fuck you" Supreme said as he pressed the end button on his phone and tossed it in the cup holder.

They passed through Denver and started up the Rockies. Scoop honked the horn when he was pulling up on Supreme.

"Do we gotta drive all the way to the top of this bitch? There aint no rails to stop you from flying off this bitch. Tell the nigga to slow down." Scoop swerved and Justice screamed like a little bitch.

"Quit playing, we dirty, we dirty, we ridin dirty!"

"You just scared nigga, admit it."

"I aint scared," Scoop swerved again,

"Ok, ok, I'm scared, I'm scared."

Scoop phone rang, "what's up?"

"Why the fuck yall keep swerving back there?"

"Fucking with this scary ass nigga."

"Quit playing, we eight and a half hours away. Let's make it to where we going."

"Alright, that's Katrina! Imma hit you back."

"What's up baby,"

"Hey! You okay?"

"Yeah, we passin through these mountains in Colorado. I wish you was riding with me. You would love this scenery."

"Where Supreme and Justice" Justice right here" he looked over at him.

"You bet not say shit about me being scared." he whispered.

"Did I hear him say he was scared?" Scoop broke out laughing,

"You told on yourself, she heard you. You should see this shit babe, we on the seventy, up here in the mountains aint no guard rails, so a nigga could just drive right off the side."

"Well you need to pay attention to the road, so I'm gonna let you go. Be careful I love you Scoop!"

"I love you too baby."

"Make sure you call me as soon as you make it." I got you babe." They both hung up.

$ $ $ $ $

Katrina drove past the house just to make sure everything was in place. It was four in the afternoon in Detroit and she didn't have anything else to do, so she drove to the Eastside to go holla at her brother.

Katrina pulled up on Mack St., parked her car two houses down from their main trap spot. As she walked up the steps all eyes were on her, as her ass shook through the tights, she wore with her Giuseppe Zanotti heels. It wasn't hot out, but it was starting to warm up. She walked through the door into the living room.

"What's good Katrina?"

"What's up Scooter? Where my brother at?" she said. "He upstairs."

She walked past and Scooter couldn't help but to look at her. Katrina had an ass like Jackie O, but everything else was her own, she was the replica of Aaliyah's song "One in a million."

"What's up brother? What are you doing?"

"What's good lil sis? I aint doing shit. What's on your mind?"

"I was thinking about flying to Las Vegas and meeting Scoop out there."

"What is he doing in Vegas?"

"He went to go meet up with his cousin out there and have some fun."

"Did he ask you to come?"

"In so many words yes, but he's not out there yet. They about eight hours away. He didn't want me to ride because of the dope in the car."

"So, they traffickin dope all the way to the west coast?"

"Yeah, but they two cars deep, and he's not in

the car with the dope, he's in the decoy car. You should have heard how they planned it, its fool proof."

"That nigga really about his bread aint he? I like his drive, but I hope he's smart too." D.K Said.

So, if you're trying to fly out there. Why you over here?"

"I was wanting to tell you and see what you think."

"Trina, that's your man, and you're not a little girl anymore. If you want to do something, just do it. You are always going to be my sister and I'm always going to have your back, 'Dion and Katrina', we all we got" they said at the same time.

"Well come on" she said pulling on his arms.

"What?"

"I need you to take me to the airport."

Once they got to the airport Katrina was ready to go, she was anxious, and excited to be going to Las Vegas. The only place she can remember going to was New York City, when DK took her for her 21st birthday.

"You need help with your bags?"

"What bags?" she said.

"You aint taking shit with you?"

"Just the cash you gave me, and the thong on my ass!"

"Girl you crazy!"

"I'm going to shop while I'm out there." she said.

"Well you know what to do if you need something. You want me to walk you to the gate?"

"I'm okay, but don't be having none of your bucket head hoes fucking and sucking in my car. I just got it detailed."

"Bye Felicia" DK said as she closed the door and walked into the airport.

DK turned up the radio and Gucci Mane came on blasting through the four twelves she had in the trunk. " I got so many felonies I can never go to Canada, but Drake said he going to pull some strings so let me check my calendar, I just popped me one of them what-you-Call-its and it boosted my stamina" He sang along as he Bobbed his head and pulled off into traffic.

16

It was 9:30 p.m. when Supreme, Scoop, and Justice entered Las Vegas on I-15. They could see the whole city lit up like it was Christmas. They drove nonstop. Supreme was anxious to get to where he was going. He felt like if they stopped somewhere to rest, they were giving the police a chance to catch up with them.

"Oh, shit son, this mother fucka look alive. I know they got dumb pussy floating around here. I seen on MSNBC Sin City has the most tourist in the world along with prostitution" Justice said.

"So, you talkin about paying for some pussy now nigga?" Scoop said and laughed.

"Nah, but I plan on pulling me a couple of broads and having fun. You know what happens in Vegas stays in Vegas!"

"Where we supposed to be going?" Justice

said. "Call Supreme and tell him to fall back behind us. I'm about to call Millz and see where we're going to meet this nigga at."

Millz answered on the first ring.

"What's up family" he said with his proper West Coast swag.

"What up bruh? Where are we supposed to meet you at?"

"Y'all in the city already?"

"Yeah, we on the 15, and we're coming up on Craig Road."

"All right look, you're welcome to come to my spot, or y'all might want your own space. They got these fully furnished condos that you can pay monthly, or weekly and everything included."

"Yeah, that sounds good"

"Alright, take the I-15 all the way to Flamingo West exit, and make the first left at the light and pull in those first Apartments you see. I'll be there in like 10 minutes. I'll get the spot in my name, and you can just shoot me the cash back when you get here."

"All right, that's a bet." Scoop said.

They pulled up to the Palisades about 30 minutes later and they parked in front of the office.

He called Millz. "We just pulled up, where you at?" Scoop said.

"That you in that blue Challenger? I'm right here in the white Benz!"

Millz and Scoop got out at the same time, "Aww shit what's up fam!", they shook hands and embraced each other. They took a step back and looked at each other.

"You look good bro, all fresh and fly, and that's your whip? damn nigga what you doing? Robbing banks now? I never thought you was going to get out the D!"

"Yeah, I had to do something. But fuck that, where you get that Benz from?"

"You know just a little something I've been saving for."

Justice got out the car, aww shit is that Mikael? What the fuck, I aint seen you in forever"

"I know fam but check this out before we go any further…. Everybody calls me Millz or Milly! Short for Millions. I don't need none of these nigga's or hoes knowing my government, you feel me."

"I got you."

They shook hands and embraced as well. "Supreme in the truck right there. That nigga probably rolling up some dro. We ain't smoked shit the whole way here."

Millz ran over to the driver side of the Tahoe and put his hand up like he was holding a gun. Supreme seen him out the corner of his eye and reached on his waist. There was no pistol there for him to grab.

"Fuck" he thought. Millz pulled the door open.

"What's up fam?" Supreme looked and looked again.

"What's up wit it M?" He said excited.

"You playing and shit, you lucky I ain't have my heat on me."

Millz laughed "Same old Supreme." they shook hands.

"Let's go around to the spot and we can smoke up there. Pull your truck around, y'all follow me."

Mills jumped into the S65 V12 Benz and pulled around to the back. The spot was upstairs and had a clear view of the strip from the balcony. They grabbed all their bags and followed Millz up to the apartment. He opened the door with the key, and they all walked in.

To be a fully furnished apartment, it was laced up. Black leather couch, with a matching loveseat, a table in the living room with a 46-inch flat screen on the wall. High seated glass dining room table. There were matching lamps on the end tables, and the kitchen had brand new dishes, pots, and pans.

There were three bedrooms, they all have queen size beds, there was only one room that had the bathroom separate.

"I don't know how y'all going to pick rooms but y'all can worry about that later. Spark that loud up Supreme, let me see what you're working with."

They all sat at the dining room table passing a blunt around.

"So, what really brought you all out here?"

"We wanted to check the city out! To see if they lived up to the hype, why we had the money to come, and we wanted to check out the hustle game out here. Is it all fast money out here?" Scoop asked.

"Depends on what kind of fast money you trying to get. It ain't the crack game like back in Detroit. It's either, crystal meth, cocaine, or Molly out here."

The blunt finally got around to Millz, and he took a long hit on the blunt, he didn't even cough. He passed it to Justice who was sitting to the right of him.

"That's some alright." Millz came out the pocket with a pack of swisher sweets. There were three blunts already Rolled up. Millz lit one, and hit it hard, he started to choke as he held the smoke in, he passed the blunt to the left. Scoop tried to take a big hit, and as he inhaled, he began to choke.

"Ah Ahh, ahhh, ahhh! What is this?" He pushed out.

"That's that O.G Kush, straight outta Cali. Don't let it burn! Pass the dutchie to the left-hand side nigga!" He said as he laughed.

They all hit the blunt and was high as Astronaut shit and sat at the table bull shitting with each other.

"How much was this spot? How much we owe you?" Justice asked.

"It's twelve hundred with a three-hundred-dollar deposit." He pulled out the receipt and put it on the table with the keys. Scoop, Supreme, and Justice all counted out five hundred each and gave it to Millz.

"We appreciate it."

"Don't mention it, we family. I got some runs to make, but if yall tryna hit the club tonight hit me up around one a.m."

"What time the club close out here?" "Around six, but it don't get to Poppin until around twelve thirty or one, and the afterhours from six to ten at Drai's Nightclub."

"Man, this city never sleeps, real talk."

"We gonna chill tonight, but what's up with some of that O.G?" Supreme asked.

They were exhausted from the nonstop drive, but Justice was ready to move around. He was the only one who got any sleep. Millz tossed the two sweets on the table just as Supremes phone began to ring. It was Katrina.

"I'm gone give my weed connect your number and he gone hit you up in a few. His name Ace, he playa so don't trip."

"Aight." Scoop said as he answered the phone.

"What's up baby?"

"What's up? I see you forgot to call me already huh?"

"Nah we just got to the spot, we ain't even figure out the rooms yet, but what's up? What are you doing? Where you at?" she laughed.

"What's funny?"

"You aint gone believe me if I told you."

"Sure, I will. I thought we were better than that?"

"I'm shopping!"

"Ain't nowhere in the D open right now, I see you want to play with my emotions!"

"Aww look at baby. Do you think if I was doing something wrong, I would call you? Anyways, where you staying at?"

"In some condo by this casino called the Rio."

"What's the address? I gotta make sure you aint fuckin with none of them hoes out there!"

"And how you gone do that?"

"Boy just give me the address! Text it to me and I'll call you back when I get it, but until then I'm hanging up the phone." Katrina hung up.

"I know she aint hang up. This girl crazy trippin."

"What's up bruh?" Justice said.

"Nothing," he grabbed the receipt that Millz left on the table and texted the address off the top of the paper.

"I don't know what's wrong with women these days." He said and sighed.

$ $ $ $ $

Katrina was already in a cab heading toward the Rio. She was still wearing her outfit from earlier and had a few bags from Coco Chanel and Chinese Laundry. She has never seen so many high-end stores before, except the time she was in New York, but DK didn't give her enough time to shop. This time she was sure she was going to see every store, every dress, and all the heels before she left the city, and she wanted to go back to Detroit with all new shit before it even made it out there!

The address popped up in her text messages a few minutes later, and she put it in her GPS, it was about five minutes away. The taxi driver picked her up from Planet Hollywood. He tried to take her the long way to make a couple extra dollars, but that didn't work.

"Make a left at the next light up there."

"I thought you said go to Rio?"

"No, I stay right over there" as she pointed. "It's just easier to say the Rio. Everyone knows where it is at." she freestyled.

"Ok." The driver said. The light turned green and they made a left turn on Dean Martin Dr. "Right here, turn in here." He pulled into the condos. The meter read 11.80, she pulled out a twenty and let him keep the change. He jumped out and opened the door for her.

"You ever need a taxi, I'll drive you anywhere u want to go" he said with his strong middle eastern accent, handing her his card.

"I will make sure of that. Thank you" Katrina said. He got back into the taxi and sat there for a minute watching her ass as she walked off.

"So Beautiful" he said to himself.

She stopped, turned around and looked at him, hoping he would get the point to drive off. He put the car in reverse, backed out of the parking spot, changed gears, looked one last time, and drove off. "Allah Akbar" he said.

Katrina was looking up on the building signs and seen she was going in the right direction. She got to building twenty-three and looked at the doors. She walked up the stairs carrying her bags to apartment 2305. She knocked on the door as she placed her finger over the peep hole so they couldn't see out.

Justice got up and opened the door, not even bothering to ask who it was or look out the peephole.

"What the?"

"Shhh" she said, as she held her index finger over her lips and walked through the door "SURPRISE!" Katrina yelled as she seen Scoop sitting on the couch watching TV

"What the fuck?" he said as he got up off the couch and gave her a hug picking her up in the air and squeezing her.

"Yall act like yall aint seen each other in years." Justice said, as he closed and locked the door. They kissed as he grabbed on her ass.

"I thought you was illin me."

"Boy stop, I'm right here by your side, that should tell you something. I had to get the address without you knowing so I could surprise you!"

"How long you been out here?"

"I got on the 7 o'clock flight out of Detroit and got here about seven forty-five p.m. but I aint make it to the strip until eight thirty and I was gone get a room, but I started shopping! I aint know they had designer stores in the casino's!"

"Shit, me either. Oh, look babe" he pulled the half a blunt out the ashtray and lit it, took a hit and handed it to her.

She hit it like she always did, and began to cough up a lung, she dropped the blunt trying to catch her breath.

"What the fuck is that?" she said as she wiped her eyes and nose. Supreme was laughing his ass off.

"That's the real shit! OG Kush from Cali."

"Fuck, where this shit been, my whole life! I'm high as shit, and I only hit it once."

"Yeah, the nigga on his way over here to sell us a zip of this shit"

"Well, come get me and Scoop when he gets here with the smoke. Y'all ain't got no bottles of drank?" She asked. That one hit put her in the mood to please her man and get pleased also. But she had it on her mind the whole plane ride.

They went to the room on the right and closed the door, it was one with the bathroom. She popped her bra off and dropped it on the floor, then kicked off her heels. She turned and faced her fat ass towards Scoop, bent over as she was pulling her leggings off, and her ass was bouncing as she kicked the last of them off her ankles. She walked towards Scoop who was sitting on the bed enjoying everything about his woman, she placed both her hands on his legs and dropped down to her knees.

17

Scoop went to go meet up with this guy he met at the 7-Eleven to make a drug deal. He pulled up on a residential street and dialed the guy's number "Where are you?" Scoop asked. "I'm pulling up behind you right now." Scoop looked in the rear-view mirror, a white Toyota Camry parked behind him, and the guy got out of the driver's seat, and walked up on the passenger side of Scoops Challenger and got in.

"What's the deal?" The guy said as he shook Scoops hand.

"You got the bread?" Scoop said. The guy reached in his left jacket pocket and pulled out a neat stack of hundreds and gave them to Scoop.

"It's all there." He said.

Scoop Counted out eighteen thousand dollars, he reached under the driver's seat and pulled out a plastic bag and handed it to the guy in the passenger seat. He opened the bag, pulled the tape off the half of brick, and took a bump of the cocaine, and rub his fingers over his gums and his mouth went numb.

"Yeah that's that shit" he said he pulled up his jacket and stuffed the dope in his pants and put his right hand into his jacket pocket and gripped the gun without revealing it. He pulled the trigger 2 times hitting him in his chest and torso. The guy grabbed the money that he gave Scoop for the dope, and exited the vehicle while Scoop struggle to breathe, bleeding from his stomach and chest. He got into his car and pulled off.

Scoop woke up, taking a deep breath drenched in sweat, as he rubbed his hands across his chest and stomach, checking for bullet wounds.

"Are you alright baby?" Katrina said.

"Yeah, I'm good."

He laid back on the pillow, and Katrina pushed herself closer and tried to comfort him. She knew something was bothering him but decided not to press the issue. She knew when he was ready, he would tell her.

He laid back pondering what that dream could have meant. He closed his eyes and tried to relax, a few minutes later he had fallen back to sleep.

$ $ $ $

Supreme and Justice decided to check out the strip, they both got fitted, and rolled a few blunts and headed out. They rode in Supremes Tahoe, and turned onto Las Vegas Blvd. They passed the Flamingo hotel and Casino and spotted woman after woman in little dresses, high heels, and a whole lot of sex appeal.

"Ohhh shit! I got to get me one of them." Supreme said excitedly.

"Shit pull up and lets Valet at the Quad, and we can go check a few of them dimes." Justice said.

Supreme pulled into the hotel and they both got out of the truck. They tipped the guy working Valet a twenty-dollar bill and they headed into the Casino. Now this was a whole different atmosphere compared to the Casinos in Detroit. One hundred percent luxury, with all different types of women dancing on platforms and poles above the blackjack tables.

There were women everywhere, some with their girlfriends, and others with their husbands, and boyfriends.

"Let's stop at the bar and get a drink." Justice said.

"I'm down, then we gone go pull a couple of hoes. I'm in need of some good head!" Supreme said as they both laughed and strolled to the bar with a swagger no man has matched tonight.

They both seemed extremely confident and knew what they wanted. The bartender approached them "What can I get you two handsome fellas?"

She was a white blue-eyed barbie that stood six foot with heels. She knew how to rock her mini skirt and lace stockings. She was the finest white chick either of them has seen in person.

"Shit if I can get you in a stiffler I wouldn't need anything else." Supreme said.

She smiled and looked toward Justice.

"Two double shots of Remy X.O straight up."

"I could look at you both and tell that ya'll have good taste!"

"And how could you tell that?"

"Just by looking at your clothes and shoes! Aren't those Theodore frames?"

"I guess you do know good taste."

"Yeah, I'm high on fashion" she said as she slid their drinks to them. "eighty-four fifty."

Supreme pulled out a bank roll and dropped a hundred-dollar bill on the bar trying to impress the bartender, "do you have a pen I can use?"

She grabbed a pen that was next to the cash register and handed it to him. Supreme took the napkin and wrote his cell phone number on it and left it on the bar.

"Call me if you want to find out what elegance from a hood nigga with money feels like." Supreme picked up his drink took a sip and turned and they both walked away.

"You really think that white bitch gone call you?" Justice asked. "I know she gone call; didn't you see the way she was looking at me? White hoes go after what's attractive to them, swag, money, muscles, and chocolate is a white chicks dream."

Justice laughed, "and don't forget that BBC."

"And where the hell did you hear that?"

"Look at the little bitch Miley, she loves some black dick. Shit, I know all the hoes heard once they go black, they'll never go back and just that right there will make her want to try me."

"I guess, but I'm trying to find me something I can hit tonight" Justice said.

They walked out of the casino and onto the street where the foot traffic looked like New York City in the morning. It was two am and the streets were still packed with drunk tourists enjoying themselves.

A sexy slim thick Latina was strolling in their direction, moving through the pedestrians with a smooth bounce in her step as her breast pushed up from her Victoria Secret bra that helped expose more cleavage than necessary. Her red leather Dior mini skirt rose up her bare toned legs exposing her black lace thong with every step.

Justice spotted her and stopped in mid stride looking so hard he could of ran over everyone that came across his path. He took a sip of his cognac as he admired everything about her. Supreme noticed that Justice wasn't beside him, so he turned around to look for him, and he seen what he was staring at. Supreme smiled and watched as Justice took a step-in front of her as she tried to walk past. They bumped into each other and she dropped her drink onto Justices Mauri Gator tennis shoes. He looked down at his kicks then back up at her. "Excuse me, I'm so sorry about that" she said as she tried to walk away with her head down trying to avoid eye contact. Justice grabbed her by the arm. That's all you got to say?" He said. She stood there with her head down. Justice pushed her chin up gently so that they were staring into each other's eyes.

"You could at least have a drink with me for ruining my $1,000 shoes", she smiled.

Justice forget all about Supreme and walked into "The Pit". There was music blasting and people dancing, but he didn't see anyone but her. They grabbed a seat at the bar. "What would you like?" he asked her.

"Patron and Pineapple"

"And a shot of Remy XO" they told the bartender.

As they waited for their drinks Justice admired everything about her.

"What's your name?"

"Lily" she said. The bartender set their drinks on the counter And Justice paid from the stack of twenties he pulled out.

"I'm Justice" he said as he took a sip and extended his arm.

She looked down unable to hold his stare. she uncrossed her legs and grabbed her drink and took a big gulp. He didn't notice it because he was caught up looking between her legs. Her juice box was so fat. Amber Rose had nothing on her in her black lace

Victoria Secret panties. She put her hands in between her legs and rubbed two fingers over her pussy. Justice looked up and she was smiling.

"You want to go back to my room?" she said.

Justice took the glass and drowned it in one swallow. He took a step closer to her so she could smell his cologne, he leaned in and put his lips right next to her ear and licked her neck.

"Let's go" he said as he rubbed his hand over her panties and felt that wet wet. She stood up and grabbed Justices hand, and they began to converse as they walked.

$ $ $ $ $

Supreme got a text message.

"If you're still close by, come meet me back at the bar. Jennifer!" He headed back toward the quad Hotel and Casino.

18

Millz called Scoop around two. Scoop allowed his phone to ring a few times before he answered. "What's up Kinfolk", Scoop said, "I was checking to see if y'all wanted to slide through my hood BBQ. It's going to be poppin and I can introduce you to a few of my A1 from day 1 niggas.

"Yeah sure I'm down. I'm going to tell Justice and Supreme and we'll slide through".

"That's a bet family. There's already people showing up but it don't officially start until 3:30".

"We'll be there"

"I am about to text you the address".

"That's a bet I'll call you when we're pulling up". Scoop pressed the screen and ended the call. Who was that baby?"

"My cousin, he just invited us to a barbecue. So,

get dressed babe we're going to go see how they do it out here on the West Coast.

Scoop walked to the living room and supreme was rolling a blunt of that OG Kush.

"Okay, I'm right on time". Supreme looked up with a smile on his face and tossed him a blunt that he already rolled up.

"Spark that".

"Millz just called me and invited us to the hood BBQ. He said it was going to be jumpin so let's go see what they about and try to turn some heads".

"You know I'm with that, and later on Justice can tell you about our night", Supreme said and laughed.

"What you mean? Where y'all go?"

"Sure, why you were doing your thing we checked out the strip. Justice knocked a super bad ass Mexican bitch and left me. And I'm glad he did cause I hooked up with this white chick who works as a bartender. I had her squealing like a pig. She was thick, and kind of reminded me of that model Ashley Graham, but she was way more tone",

"You fucked a white chick? Yeah right!"

"Shit, I got it on video. She a freak 2" Supreme went to the video and handed the phone to Scoop as he hit the blunt.

His boy couldn't believe what he saw. Scoop was impressed. Jennifer had ass like Serena, and she knew how to twerk. She bent over and he could see her pussy from the back.

"I know bro and she trying to kick it with me tonight cause she off work".

"Where is justice?"

"He should be gettin out the shower"

"Come on, let's sneak in on this nigga and see what he is doing".

They both got up and slid into Justices room. The water was still running. They crept to the bathroom that was connected to his room, "aaaahhhh!" Supreme caused Justice to holla and fall in the shower. They both laughed and slid back the curtain.

"What the fuck y'all doing in here?"

"Shit you was taking forever so we came here to check on you. Dry off and get fly, we about to head to the barbecue with Millz, and there's supposed to be a bunch of pussy there" Scoop said.

"I'm with that. Let me hit that blunt, shit. I need to calm my heart rate now, muthafucka scared the shit out of me".

Justice turned the water off and took the piece of blunt and put it to his mouth as they walked out. Justice finished smoking the doobie as he got out the shower and dried off.

$ $ $ $ $

Scoop and Katrina pulled up in the Challenger and Supreme and Justice behind them in the Tahoe. They all got out looking like a fashion show in Paris.

Supreme and Justice grabbed the bottles of liquor out the backseat as Scoop answered his phone.

"What's up family?" Millz said as he answered his phone.

"We just pulled up and parked."

"Aight, we are by the basketball court. You'll see us, everyone is wearing white T's with green trees on the front of them."

"Aight we are walking up now"

"Cool, I'll keep an eye out for you."

There were kids running around everywhere playing in the water. There was a full court basketball game going on with people waiting on the side, some waiting to play and some making bets. When the four of them walked up, there were groups of people chilling, smoking, drinking, playing spades, dominoes, and shooting dice.

Millz was standing by a table that had a few women sitting and eating. He turned and spotted his family and walked over to them.

'What's the deal?" Millz said as he gave Scoop, Justice, and Supreme a handshake with a half hug.

"We bought a few bottles, you know we aint want to come empty handed".

"That's cool, come on let me introduce you all to a few people. But first who is this black Queen on your arm Scoop?"

"This is my woman Katrina" he said as she smiled.

"How are you doing Katrina?" Millz said as he

stuck out his hand, "I'm his older cousin Millz".

"Nice to meet you!"

They walked under the shade tree where the picnic tables were, and they sat down. Millz called two of his best friends over and introduced them all.

They all sat down and started talking, they poured drinks, and rolled several blunts. Everyone was enjoying themselves. Out of nowhere the was an argument that broke out in swinging fist and hair pulling.

Millz realize who it was and got up from the bench and pulled the two women apart and made them chill out. Frog and Jizzle stayed at the table to talk to Supreme Scoop and Justice.

"So, what be selling out here? What's the main hustle?" Supreme asked.

"Shit, that white girl…." Frog said.

"Are you talking about white girls or cocaine?" Justice asked.

"Shit pimping and hoeing are always going to be number one, but that cocaine is a pimp and a hoes best friend. Cocaine, cocaine is the hustle… We been stopped selling crack. That soft money is way better."

"Oh yeah? So, what the ounces and grams go for?" Supreme asked.

"fifty a gram eight hundred an ounce, and if it's that pure shit you can get a stack for a twenty-eight if you know what I'm saying…"

"We might have to link up soon. We gone holla

at Millz and plug in with yall!"

"That's a bet. We can do something" Frog said.

Millz came back over and sat down at the table, "I don't know why these females be trippin like that…"

Shit I don't either, but Meme got her ass whooped!" Jizzle said as everyone broke out into laughter.

"We were just talking business over here, and we might need to get down with yall A.S.A.P. so we can get to the money."

"What y'all trying to do?" Millz asked.

"The same shit we were doing back home, but they said powder is the money maker out here."

"Yeah, the young niggas in the hood we let them sale the crack, and we make them big boy sales. You know just supply them with that and the people with the real bread the soft. But let's talk business another time. Let's enjoy this Barbeque!" Millz said.

They all agreed that they would talk later. They chilled until it got dark, then everyone got ready to go. Scoop, Supreme, and Justice shook everyone's hand and headed back to their spot.

19

The next day came around and Justice was in the kitchen stretching the cocaine. They knew if they were going to make any money out in Las Vegas they were going to have to stretch the product. The price difference was a large gap compared to what they were making back in Detroit.

Justice made one brick into two, compressed it, wrapped it in plastic then tossed them into the freezer.

Millz showed up to the spot dressed to impress like always. He stepped into the apartment wearing a silk Versace shirt, robin jeans, and some black Versace loafers with the gold Medusa head on them. He wore a nice custom Breitling watch, with a pair of wood framed Cartier glasses. Supreme was digging Millz style, he knew he could take a few pointers from him.

"What's up family?" Millz said.

"You know we just trying to make a dollar out of fifteen cents."

"Take a look at this and tell me what you think?" Scoop said as he tossed him a sandwich bag with a few grams of coke in it.

Millz looked at it in the light, "you mind if I try it?"

"Be my guest!" Scoop said.

Millz took his pinky nail and stuck it in the bag and pulled out a bump, he held it up to his nostril and inhaled, and he took another bump with the opposite nostril. He tipped his head back and wiped his nose with his index finger and thumb, and waited a minute for it to kick in.

The cocaine began to drip down his throat and began to numb his throat tongue and face.

"That's some good shit. Y'all brought this with ya'll?"

"Yeah, we got a lil bit with us. You think it will move out here?" Scoop said

"I ain't even gone bullshit y'all cause yall family, but this is the best shit that I have come across in a while."

"You think you can help us move this brick?"

"How much y'all asking for?"

"Twenty-eight!"

"Is it the same shit?"

"It's the exact same shit!" Scoop said

"Yeah I can have that whole thing sold in one

phone call" Millz said as he pulled out his iPhone. Scoop nodded at Justice and he went and got one of the bricks out the freezer.

"No need to make that phone call, just do what you need to do and bring back the bankroll" Scoop said as Justice tossed the brick of cocaine to Millz.

"That's what's up give me an hour and I'll have the money back over here. Give or take five minutes…"

"No need to rush I know you good for it" Scoop said.

"Well let me go get to it, I'll be on your line in a minute".

"It's love" Supreme said. Millz put the kilo in his pants and pulled his Versace shirt over his jeans and walked out the door.

"You think we should have put a whole brick in his hand? We ain't been around him in years. That's why I had you stretch one so we can see if he's still trustworthy. We ain't losing shit if he don't come back. Plus, this nigga knows the whole city, and he's doing well for himself. I looked up that Benz he was whipping and that bitch cost one hundred and seventy thousand basic and his was souped up. If he brings the money back, and they like that shit we back in business."

"I feel you" Justice said.

"Shit what we gone do until then?" Supreme asked.

"Roll up some of that Kush and let go

shopping!"

$ $ $ $ $

Back at Cedar Sinai Hospital, Dunk was lying in a bed with tubes down his throat, in a coma. He suffered from severe blood loss, and one of his lungs stopped working so they had to remove it.

He had been shot three times twice in the chest and one in the abdomen.

The hospital was talking about sending him to hospice because they didn't know if he was going to recover. Dunk's best friend was sitting next to the bed when he opened his eyes. He looked around and didn't know where he was. He began pulling at the tubes and IVs that were attached to him. Pete stood up from his chair.

"Oh shit. You woke up, you woke up. Calm down calm down. I got you bruh... NURSE, NURSE!" Pete yelled as he held Dunks arms trying to calm him down.

They rushed in, "oh, God! He woke up let me get the doctor."

"Mr. Grady I'm going to ask you a few questions, blink once for yes and twice for no. Do you understand?" Dunk blinked once. "That's good, are you in any pain?"

He blinked once and pointed at the tube in his throat. "Okay, we will take the tube out very soon just hang in there. Do you know what happened to

125

you?" Dunk blinked twice.

"Ok, can you wiggle your toes for me?"

The doctor pulled up the blanket, so Dunk's toes were showing, he blinked his eyes once, but his toes didn't move.

"Can you move your toes for me again?" Dunk tried for the second time and his toes began to move.

The doctor took his hand and squeezed Dunk's right foot.

"Can you feel that?" He blinked once again. "Ok, that's very good. We are going to get this tube out of you and get you a little more comfortable. Then we are going to send you back to ICU and run a few more test on you. But this tube will be out of you in less than an hour."

Pete was excited that his friend was awake and going to be okay, he wanted to question him and see if he remembered anything, but first Dunk would need to get the tubes out of him and finished with his test. Pete wanted revenge for his friend's sake, but more so it gave him a reason to use his twins.

$ $ $ $ $

Scoop, Katrina, Supreme and Justice walked back into the apartment with multiple bags. Everyone was feeling good, they all put their bags up and came back into the living room.

Scoop's phone rang, he answered it.

"Open the door family, I'm coming up the

stairs."

When Millz walked into the living room he tossed thirty grand onto the table.

"That's thirty G's right there", he said as he pulled up a chair from the dining room. Supreme pulled the rubber bands off the three stacks of hundreds and began counting. There were one hundred, hundred-dollar bills in each stack, he counted out two grand and handed it to Millz.

"I appreciate it family."

"Nah, we appreciate you."

"I sold it for thirty bandz, but I know we can make a lot more if we break them down. If I calculated this right, fourteen hundred an ounce, thirty-six ounces, we can get fifty grand minimum." Millz said.

"And how are we supposed to get the clientele." Justice asked.

I already got the clientele. All we gotta do is get a trap house, and I'll let everyone know it's a gram spot. But you gone need a couple youngstas pushing it, that way you don't have to take any chances. And I got two little homeboys that hustle hard and will fire that heat if they got too."

"We can do that asap, but do you know any places that would be a good spot?"

"I'll set that up, but what am I gone need to do to get a cut of the play? Millz asked.

"You don't need to do anything, just do what you said, and you gone get a cut bruh. Ya feel   me?"

"Yeah, I feel you, I can have the spot in a few days."

"That's a bet. Just let us know and we'll be ready."

"Aight" Millz said.

Millz slid out the door as he tucked the two grand into his pocket, and gracefully made his way to his car with more money on his mind. See, Millz was already a big player in the game of pimps and hoes. But he seen a chance to extend his income and build his empire at a faster rate, without getting his hands dirty. He couldn't pass up that opportunity.

Millz use to sell dope but was introduced to a new hustle when he touched down in Sin City. An ol' skool pimp took a liking to him. So, he took him under his wing and began teaching him the ropes of the game. He also gave him his first hoe and blessed him with his handle, which was his nickname that he went by. Once he committed himself to the game he took off and never looked back. That was ten years ago, and he was at the top of his game, in his prime.

Millz knew that Scoop, Supreme, and Justice had to have a lot more dope, if they were willing to just put a whole brick in his hands and not worry about it. It's been many of years since they spent any time with each other, but he knew what Scoop was capable of. He knew that he would rather have the trio on his side then to be against them. Selling dope wasn't part of Millz hustle anymore, but he had a hood full of youngstas that were loyal to him, that were ready for anything on the drop of a dime.

He sent out a few text messages as he checked backpage for a rental property that they could use to trap out of. He knew if he found a spot close to the strip, they would make a lot of fast money 24/7. Las Vegas is the city that never sleeps, and the cocaine is what helps keep the city awoke.

A few hours later Millz was meeting up with a couple that was going to be renting him a double wide trailer off W. Tropicana. He gave the owners five hundred dollars for the first moth with a hundred- and fifty-dollar deposit. Millz pulled out the grocery store parking lot and drove across the street to check out the trailers and the community. It was one of the nicer trailers in the area. He looked around and there was a lot going on.

Millz knew this was the spot to be in. And it was only a hop skip and a jump away from the strip. He made the call and gave a few of the little homies a job to do as we got into his Benz. He told them what needed to be done and he would make sure their pockets weren't hurting anymore.

20

Dunk was out of the hospital and on a mission to find out who was behind him being shot and robbed. He wanted blood, so he called a meeting with his team who hustled over on Plymouth and greenfield. He spoke to his number two guy and found out that he was robbed by three guys also. Dunk knew it wasn't a coincidence. His #2 came in contact three different times with these guys and still had his life. That was uncommon for a guy who had problems with the trio.

Keno stopped looking for the three guys when he escaped with his life after leaving the club. He wasn't just dealing with three average cats. He had to worry about a whole team of killers. MSG was not to be fucked with. The proof of that was his three boys laying in caskets 6 feet under, and five of his boy's bodies riddled with bullets. Not one of them seen it coming.

Keno didn't want any parts of what Dunk was planning. He barely escaped deaths grip, and he didn't plan on dying anytime soon. He knew death didn't like to be cheated, and he knew if he kept playing with fire he was eventually going to get burned.

"The niggas that robbed you, do you remember what they looked like? Everything happened so fast, but I do remember one of them. Man look Dunk I don't think you should go looking for these niggaz. They over a hundred deep and what makes it worse, D KING from Mack St, said they are his brothers."

"I don't give a fuck if they were apostles from the bible. I'm gone hunt each one of them down and make them feel my pain. These got to be the niggas that hit me. I'm gone have to sit down with D KING."

"I advise you not to do that. This nigga put a hit on me, and he don't know I'm still breathing. If he finds out I'm as good as dead. Just leave it alone. If you don't you might not live to see your next birthday. They let us leave the club and nobody followed us out. And somehow, they managed to still pull up on us and ripped both the whips to shreds. Ark, Boobie, and Lil Jesse are dead."

"And you just gone let these niggas get away with that? You sound like a pussy right now"

"I escaped with my life. I have two boys that need they dad, and there is nothing more important than that."

"I can't believe you right now" Dunk said as he turned and walked out the house. "Good luck with your future." Dunk closed the door behind him and slid into the passenger seat of his Range Rover wishing he didn't hear what Keno just told him.

Dunk was determined to get even. He knew before he got shot that his head was in between Katrina's legs. He didn't know what happened to her. He doubted that she had anything to do with the robbery, but he wanted to make sure she was ok.

Dunk dialed Katrina's number, and the phone began to ring. He held the phone to his ear waiting for an answer.

$ $ $ $ $

Katrina looked at the screen of her cell phone, and the call was coming from Dunk. She couldn't believe what she was seeing. Katrina thought he was dead. She didn't know what to do.

"Who is that baby?" Scooped asked as he came from the kitchen smoking a blunt.

"It's Dunk" she said shocked.

"The nigga we robbed?" he asked.

"Yes, him!"

"Well answer the phone and see what he says."

Katrina answered the call, "Hello?"

"Katrina, what's up?"

"Who is this?"

"So, you aint ever lock my number in your

132

phone? It's all good. This Dunk! I was calling to make sure everything was okay after what had happened."

"Dunk, oh my God you're okay!"

"Yeah, I'm fine shawty. The doctors say I'm blessed to make it."

"I'm sorry so sorry. I didn't know what to do." She put on a good act, "I ran out the front door and called for the police from the neighbor's phone. I was so scared I didn't know what else to do."

She sounded so sincere, she had Dunk wrapped around her finger. He couldn't remember how he got to the hospital but if the ambulance was called, he surely would have ended up dead.

"When can I see you? Dunk asked.

"I don't believe that's a good idea. I'm trying to get over what you put me thru. I could have lost my life, could have got raped, kidnapped or anything. And I should have never been at your house in the first place. That's one of the reasons I never dated a hustler. So no, I can't see you. I'm glad you are okay, but no I'm not, I can't I'm sorry." And she pressed end on her cell phone.

Katrina didn't get a bad vibe from him, but she was uncomfortable. She didn't really think about Dunk at all, but now she wouldn't be comfortable until he was dead.

"Everything is going to be okay. He doesn't have a clue of what happened."

"Well why do you think he called me after all this time?

"I'm pretty sure he just wanted to make sure you were okay. He didn't want to feel guilty, and I'm sure the last thing he remember was you. Shit to die in between your legs would be the sweetest death to me!" Scoop said as he began to rub Katrina's inner thigh. They both smiled.

$ $ $ $ $

Dunk stared at the screen of his phone with so many thoughts running through his mind. He was hurt and confused. Bringing Katrina to his house put her life in the crossfire of all the beef he had in the streets. But if she wouldn't have been there, he would have surely been resting six feet under. He didn't want to bring her anymore hurt or pain. So, he decided then and there to let the woman he fell in love with slide through his fingers. But he was even more determined to find the niggas that set these plays in motions. Their actions cost him money, his future and happiness.

"Drop me off at the house and spread the word I got twenty grand for the names of the niggas who robbed me, and I got fifty grand if they can point me in their direction."

: Are you sure you want to do that? We don't even know who these niggas are, or who's riding with them."

"Just do it. Money changes niggas loyalty, especially out here." His mind was racing as he got out of his Range Rover and walked to his house. Dunk knew he was lucky to have escaped with his life, and his money cause the safe that they got in to was only a decoy. He went to his bar poured a glass of Hennessy X.O. and relaxed in his black leather recliner.

"Let's not worry about none of that shit. I'll take care of it, we're two thousand miles away. I know he ain't gone find us out here, and he don't even know who we are. Everything is in our favor." Scoop said.

"Who's to say that he doesn't want me for setting him up?"

"He don't know what happened. He been in these streets for a while he don't know who it was. Could have been anyone, and you just so happen to be there. Ain't no way you could have set him up that fast and it went smooth like it did. That's what he is thinking."

Scoop passed the blunt of Kush to Katrina "Everything is going to be okay baby."

21

Supreme, Justice, and Millz pulled up to the trailer park, and all eyes were on them. They got the 46-inch flat screen out the trunk, with a PlayStation 4 with a bag full of games. When they walked in Jizzle, Kobe and K.T. were sitting on the couch listening to music on their phones.

Millz introduced them to his boys as Supreme pulled the tv out the box and connected the game.

Kobe looked thru the stacks of games.

"Ok, I see yall got that new Madden. Are you any good?" he asked Supreme.

"Depends on what you called good lil homie."

"Are you good enough to bet ten dollars a game" Supreme tossed Kobe a remote that was still in the packaging.

"Money on the wood keep the gambling good" Supreme said as he pulled out a bankroll full of hundreds. And dropped a $20 on the table. Kobe followed suit.

Justice and Millz were at the table with 4 ½ ounces of cocaine in front of them with 2 digital scales and a thousand little coke baggies.

"Jizzle, K.T. come here" Millz said as he motioned for them to have a seat.

Jizzle was seventeen, and aware how to bag up cocaine. He was only thirteen when he first started selling crack. The hustle was in his blood and he wouldn't hesitate to pop something if a nigga got in the way of him getting his paper.

At 19 K.T. was a real player in the hood with the young ladies. He stayed with a new fit and a pair of the latest Jordan's on his feet. He was a smart hustler, he thought about every move before he made it, and made sure he had a backup plan. He was the nigga all his boys wanted around when they were planning a lick… He had haters but they couldn't do nothing but respect him.

Now Kobe had just turned 18 and was ready to do some big things but was waiting on his opportunity, and he knew this might be it. He knew Millz was balling on a major level and he was ready to get his paper up too. Kobe had a two-year-old son and did everything to take care of him and his baby's mother. They stayed in the projects where there was no hope for most. And the Jets always had something going on, drama day in day out. Kobe was still young, but he knew he didn't want his son brought up in the projects and live a life of poverty like he did and still was.

Justice gave Jizzle a K.T. both a half ounce of cocaine.

"Bag that up by grams. Fifty a gram and four for one eighty. Yall are responsible for seven hundred dollars each. Can You handle that?" Justice asked.

"Yeah we got it" K.T. said

Kobe paused the game and walked up to the table "Shit, what y'all want me to do?"

Millz tossed him a half ounce "I thought you just wanted to play games!!!"

"Hell, nah I'm about my money too" he said as he pulled up a chair to the table and bagged up 14 baggies. Each weighing a gram.

"I'm going to leave this phone it's only for trapping don't use it for anything but that. If y'all need anything call me from your personal cell not the trap phone. And I ain't going to tell you how to hustle, but if I was you I would split up each fade you reach your one call a piece and rotate so y'all clocking and getting paid. If y'all want this to last don't serve anyone who does not call you. Can y'all do that?" Justice asked. "Yeah we got you." "and don't bring no random hoes up here."
"aight" K.T. said.

$$\$\,\$\,\$\,\$\,\$$$

Scoop was back at the spot with Katrina thinking about

how he was going to re-up on some more product.

"What do you think baby." He asked Katrina

"I think you should call Chuco and speak to him."

Scoop grabbed his phone and searched his Phone book for the plugs number and made the call. As the phone rang, he tried to get his thoughts together.

"Scoop! What's up mi amigo?"

"Chuco it's been a minute."

"AAHHHH. Not on my behalf." Chuco said

"I know I've been out of town and I'm still gone for the moment." Scoop said.

"So, where are you my friend? if you don't mind me asking!"

"I'm on the west coast doing my thing in Las Vegas."

"I see the city that never sleeps. is that true?"

"It seems to be true so far. We're just getting things started and it's looking real promising. But I need to know if there's any way"

"Stop you don't have to say it I know just give me a little time and I'll get you right. I got some family in Phoenix. So, don't worry about a thing just give me uno memento and you'll be feeling like you never left home."

"So how will it work?"

"Let me put some things together and I'll get back at you" Chuko said.

"Okay I'm cool with that." Scoop said it as he

hung up the phone.

"What did he say?" Katrina asked.

"He told me to be patient as he puts things together and he will get back to me."

"Well that wasn't so hard was it" Katrina said as she leaned over and gave her man a kiss.

$ $ $ $ $

Mary was down in the Atlanta doing her thing. She wasn't really making that much but it was enough to pay for the little one-bedroom apartment she had. When she first hit the A, she didn't know anyone and that was good for her. She knew that she could find any and everything in every city throughout the United States by the Greyhound station. So that was her first stop.

She had an ounce of crack and enough money to pay for a hotel for a month. Mary decided to check out the scenery and see if she would be able to make a few more moves. She broke off a nice piece of Dope from the Block she had and stashed the rest of it along with her money inside the rip of the passenger seat.

She grabbed her jacket out of the back seat and put it on. She got out the car that was parked directly in front of the bus station. There was a lot going on in the area, a lot of foot traffic. And just so happened to be a Monday and Magic City was jumping right across the street.

She decided to stay in visual sight of her car as she walked up and down the street. Mary wanted to call her nephew and let him know what was going on, but her conscience got the best of her. She stopped and stood in front of the payphone for a few minutes as a young boy walked up.

"Can you spare fifty cents?" He asked Mary. He looked about sixteen or seventeen years old and was dressed decently in a pair of jeans and a pullover sweater with a hood on it. His dreads hung down to his shoulders and he was kind of slim. Mary reached in her purse and pulled out a few coins and handed them over to the young man and struck up a conversation.

"Where you from shorty?" Mary asked.

"I'm from Bankhead the west side".

"What you doin down here?"

He looked at her sideways with the funny stare on his face.

"I didn't mean to offend you. We might have gotten off on the wrong foot. They call me M or Misty" Mary said.

"Rajh."

"Nice to meet you Rajh"

"Yeah you too"

"Look Rajh, I'm gone be straight up with you. I need some help and looks like you need some cash"

"What is it that you need help with?"

"Do you smoke weed?"

"Yeah" Rajh answered

"Well let's talk over a blunt of some Kush" Mary said, and he agreed as they walked toward her car that was parked in front of the Greyhound Station.

$ $ $ $ $

Supreme was at the gas station waiting in line with a black man in his mid-thirties standing behind him. Supreme stepped up to the cash register "Box of Phillies and one pack of Zig Zag longs."

"Is that all?" The cashier asked

"Fifty on that black truck." Supreme said as he collected his change and headed to pump his gas.

As the gas was pumping itself Supreme was sitting in the passenger seat with the door opener rolling a blunt. The guy from the line walked up to the truck "say family don't mean to bother you but I ain't from here and I'm in the need of some smoke."

"Where you from?" Supreme asked

"Memphis. That's my car with Tennessee plates."

Supreme looked over to the other pump and saw a Burgundy Maserati with matching rims.

"Okay, that's a nice car." Supreme finished rolling a blunt and jumped down from the passenger seat and returned the gas pump into its cradle.

"I don't sell weed, but you're welcome to smoke the blunt with me."

"Shit that's all you had to say, let's smoke!"

He got into the passenger seat of Supremes

Tahoe as they lit the blunt and pulled off.

"We gone bend a corner, so we don't attract any attention to ourselves. My name is Supreme." He said as he stuck his hand out.

"Skrilla" he said as they shook hands.

Supreme passed the blunt and Skrilla took a few hits and passed it back to Supreme.

"What brings you to Las Vegas?" Supreme asked

"The money of course."

"Same here, so what's your hustle?"

" I get that fast and easy money less risk more chips. If you know what I'm talking about? I got a few girls that work at strip club and do private parties."

"So, you a pimp?" Supreme said with a Sly grin on his face.

"That pimp word is watered down. I like to think of myself as a manager or a financial advisor. You know a word a little more professional."

"That's what's up, I grew up watching pimps in my city back in the day."

"Oh yeah, where you from?"

"Originally from Chicago but grew up in Detroit since I was eight." Supreme said

"So, what's your hustle Supreme? What do you do?"

"I'm from Detroit, so you know we shovel that snow!"

"Shit, you got some with you. I fuck around, but this other dude been hitting me over the head and his shit ain't that great."

"Yeah I got to little something" Supreme reached into the middle council and pulled out a sandwich bag with an eight ball of powder and handed it to skrilla. "Take a couple of hits and tell me what you think?"

Skrilla untied the bag and took a bump in each nostril. It took about 30 seconds to hit him.

"Oh yeah what you want for this?"

"$70 A gram 200 a ball. that's just cause of the quality. I got some shit that's cheaper but it's not as potent."

Skrilla pulled out a bank roll and gave 3 one hundred dollar bills to Supreme as he pulled back into the gas station next to the Maserati, "Hit my line whenever 24/7 we trappin" Supreme said, after he passed him his cell phone number.

"I'll probably be hitting you up tonight. My girls know a lot of these dancers that fuck around too."

"That's a bet" Skrilla exited the truck and Supreme turned up the radio, lit half the blunt that was left and drove off.

$ $ $ $ $

The trailer park was pumping cocaine. And a few trailers down they were pumping something too. There was a lot of foot traffic and most of the people were Hispanic and white.

"What's going on down there?" Kobe said as he came out and sat on the porch in between Jizzle and

K.T.

"I'm not sure but I think they sellin too, but I don't think they movin powder." K.T. said.

The Trap phone started ringing, K.T. got up to go grab it. A decent-looking white chick was walking by from the trailer down the road, and they were dying to know what was going on.

"Watch me bag this snow bunny" Kobe said.

"Excuse me" Kobe said to the white girl. She looked up at Kobe and smiled and slowed her step to see what he had to say.

"How you doin?" he asked.

"I'm fine."

"I seen you walking by a few times and I finally had enough balls to speak to you, my name is Kobe" he said as he stuck his hand out toward her, she took his hand in hers.

"I'm Katie"

"Nice to meet you. So, what you got going on? are you busy?"

"Yeah but why what's up?"

"I was just trying to see if you wanted to chill with me."

"No not today but you can call or text me. I got something to do right now. If that's alright with you?" She had her cell phone in her head.

"What's your number?" Katie asked.

Kobe grabbed her phone and dialed his number and let it ring before he handed it back.

"Why don't you call me when you're done with

what you're doing later tonight?" Kobe said.

"Okay" she said as she smiled and began to walk down the street again.

Kobe walked back to the porch and sat down next to Jizzle.

"Told you I was going to get her."

"What she say? Did you ask about who stay down there?"

"Nah I ain't ask but I'm going to find out later."

"Roll up and let's get on that new 2k. I feel like taking your money" Jizzle said as he dropped $10 onto the table.

"You ain't saying shit put up or shut up" they both laughed.

22

Now Katrina was back in Detroit, her plane had just landed as D King stood outside his Audi in passenger pick up, waiting for his sister to walk up.

He had a lot on his mind as he stood against the hood of his car. When Katrina exited the airport, he knew that was his sister the way she walked and grabbed everyone's attentions as she strolled by. He couldn't help but smile as she gave her big brother a hug.

"How was your flight?"

"It was good I had a couple glasses of wine that made it a little easier. It was smooth sailing after my second glass."

"You hungry?" D King asked

"I could go for some Coney Island."

They both got into the car and pulled off. DK

decided to wait until they finished eating to ask her about that nigga who was asking questions about her man and his two brothers. Then threw her name in the air like it was nothing.

As they ate DK tried to figure out the best approach to talk to his sister. They never had hidden anything from each other, and he didn't want her to start now.

"Trina how was your trip?"

"It was good" She said smiling.

"Well let me put you up on what's been going on out here. About a week ago a guy by the name of Dunk came by the hood asking about three guys that's always together. For some reason, my mind did not click until he mentioned your name. What's that all about?"

"I'm not sure. Dunk called me when I was in Vegas, and I told him not to call me anymore. He used to come up to the club I worked at and always threw money on me and a few of the other girls that worked there. When I wouldn't give him any play it would make him try even harder and spend even more money. Last thing I heard about him he was in the hospital from being shot."

"So why would he be coming thru the hood asking about you?"

"I don't know." Katrina said

"Katrina, I need you to be real with me right now. I don't know the intentions of this nigga, and I need to know the truth, so I know what I got to do. I can only protect you from the things I know about." DK said as he stood up "If something was to happen to you."

I don't know DK."

"This the last time I'm gone ask you, what's going on lil sis? I wouldn't be able to live with myself if something happened to you."

Katrina put her head down "He's just fishing. He doesn't even know who he is looking for."

"This nigga Dunk has a few niggas under him, and he supposed to be the head nigga from Plymouth, (P ROCK BOYS). So, tell me what's up?

"I put Scoop on the lick to rob Dunk. They said he was dead, Supreme shot him three time."

"He looked alive and well to me" D KING said.

"Well he don't know shit and he think I saved his life, so I'm not a suspect."

"How do u figure that? If this nigga is a real street nigga, he won't let that thought just slip by him. That will always be a thought in my mind."

"Well everyone ain't you DK."

"Don't even worry about it I'll take care of this nigga tonight. I'm gone send some niggas to finish the job."

"No, you can't do that. Just let him be for right now DK. I came all the way back to celebrate with you!"

"Celebrate what? That this nigga thinks you set him up?" He said in a smart tone.

"To celebrate that you're going to be an uncle!"

"What?" D KING said

"I'm Pregnant!" Katrina said

"Come again?"

"I'm pregnant, I'm going to have a baby."

"You're fucking with me, right?"

"No, you're going to be an uncle."

DK couldn't believe what he was hearing. He was happy, but the feelings he had been suppressing for the longest started to get the best of him. He tried to hold his gangsta together, but it was his baby sister, so he let it out and began to cry.

"What's a matter?" Katrina asked as she got up and pulled a chair next to her brother.

"Nothing, I just never thought I would see this day. I even prayed that Pop would at least be home by the time this happened. Me praying!!! I know that's crazy right?"

They both laughed. D.K. never had any kids of his own because he didn't trust no bitch. He knew being in this game, bitches were only good for three things 'pussy, head and an alibi'. And sometimes not even that.

He knew from experience that all these women wanted was money and more money. And he refused to be a hoes ticket out of the hood. He had at least two women for everyday of the week, and they knew the routine, Nothing more nothing less.

"I haven't told Scoop yet. I wanted you to be the first to know." D.K. Hugged his little sister and gave her a kiss on the forehead.

"Come on let's get out of here before one of these randoms see me crying." Katrina giggled and they both got up and left the restaurant.

$ $ $ $ $

Word was out on the street that there was a twenty-thousand-dollar reward for three names. The names of all the niggas who was doing the jacking around the Westside, or if anyone knew about the shooting that put Dunk in the hospital.

"What's the deal Smurf?" Dunk said Through his cell phone.

"Shit just checking with you to see if you got word on that issue you were pushing. You know about that Trio?"

"What's up? What you got for me?"

"There's these three brothers from over off 6 Mile. They're known Jack boys and word around the city, they're the ones that got you."

"Oh yeah? So how you know this? who told you?"

"Check it out, I got a lil shorty that work at the club over off 8 Mile. Said three guys came in the other night and blew a few stacks, but all the other times they used to come in and couldn't buy a drink or a dance. This time they were throwing cash like they had it. And surely even left with the bitch and two other girls that work there. They ended up getting into a shootout right after they left the club and they were the only ones that walked away."

"So, what's their names?"

"When I get that 20 G's in my hand you get the names!"

"Meet me at Walmart in Dearborn in 1 hour. Make sure the names are on point. I hate to put my money on your head too." Dunk said.

"No worries, but the info I got I know it's real. Just make sure all the money there."

Dunk walked to the floor safe in the kitchen pantry and pulled out two $10,000 stacks, all $100's and put his twin Glocks in his shoulder holsters. Poured a double shot of Remy slammed it and headed to the garage. He pulled out in the BMW M6 and headed for the freeway.

$ $ $ $ $

D.K.'s high rise condo overlooked the Detroit River and the Ambassador Bridge that entered Canada. He sat on the 21st floor with a big Philly blunt in between his fingers. He had a feeling in his gut that something wasn't right, and he knew the feeling was coming from home. He tried to shake the feeling, but it just wouldn't go away. D.K. learned a long time ago to always follow his intuition. If he didn't, he knew he was in the wrong. Reading all those Deepak Chopra books he learned how to trust himself and the feelings he had.

DK pulled his phone from his pocket and sent a

text to Scooter "Get five of the top boys and go look for that nigga Dunk. Do what you got to do but make it right. I'm going to text you the address and slide through his hood over off Plymouth and Greenfield First."

"Headed out now. We'll be in touch." Scooter said.

Katrina walked into the living room with her brother looking out over the river inhaling a big blunt of some loud. She usually enjoyed smoking with DK, but she didn't have the urge to get high anymore.

"What's on your mind bro?"

DK took another hit of the blunt and turned around.

"Just thinking I've been in the game for a long time, beat plenty of cases and I'm lucky I never ended up behind bars like pop."

"He taught you everything you know. You learn from the best."

"Yeah but he didn't know when to quit! He seen all the signs and he still chose to keep going."

"What are you saying DK? Are you thinking about getting out?"

"Not necessarily, I'm thinking about backing up, stepping out of the Limelight and not touching anything anymore. I'm thinking about putting Scooter over everything and just getting a cut of the profit. That way I'm out of the mix. I don't want to end up like pop. I've made more than enough money over the years and I want to be able to see my niece or nephew grow up. And I don't mean Behind Bars."

"What do you think the boys are going to say?"

"I'm not sure but I'm still going to treat them all like family. Hell, they are family. They are all we had since pop left."

"You can't walk out on them."

"I'm not walking out on them I'm taking my hand out of the mix, but I will always be here for them. Like I said, they're family."

DK turned back toward the window looking out over the river and took a deep hit of the blunt he was smoking. Katrina looked at his back as she regretted telling him she was pregnant. This could be the only thing that was making her brother want to get out of the game. Unless there was something, he wasn't telling her. She turned around and started down the hallway. When she entered the room, she looked at her reflection in the mirror as she placed her hand over her belly.

$ $ $ $ $

Scooter and the boys were driving around the city all day and came up with nothing. Nobody was in the hood on Plymouth, so they slid by Dunk's house and there was no sign of him there either. They passed through all the main clubs on the west side and still came up empty-handed. Scooter texted DK "no sign of him anywhere!"

"Put two niggas on the end of his street and don't let them leave until they find him." DK texted.

"Bet that"

"Meet me in the hood at 10, be dressed we're going out. Me and you!"

"I got you" Scooter said.

Scooter told two of his best shooters to stay back on dunk's block and watch for any signs of Dunk and if they see him, to take him down. He reached under the driver seat and tossed a Mac-10 with a 32-round clip to the passenger of the Impala and pulled off.

$ $ $ $ $

Dunk already met up with Smurf and the info he received was solid. He confirmed there were three brothers, known jack boys from around the six-mile area. One of the boys from over that way said they've been M.I.A. for the last three to five months. Word was they hit a nice lick and got a good connect and set up shop over on Gladstone. There was a shootout in the trap house and they ain't been seen ever since.

Dunk knew his chances of finding these niggas was slim. They were up a hundred Grand, plus two keys. They would be stupid to still be out here he thought. Dunk was desperate for Revenge. He didn't know where to start. Instead of waiting to catch the three on the rebound he decided to break the codes, morals, and ethics of the street. He pulled over and dialed 311 from a payphone and the operator came on the line.

"Detroit Police Department non-emergency line how may I help you?" The operator said.

"Yes, I would like to report some information about two shootings!"

"Please hold for a second while I transfer your call."

"Detective Whitehead how can I help you?'

"I got some info on a shooting that happened a few months back?"

"Okay what is your name?" the detective asked.

"I rather remain anonymous."

"Okay well what do you want to share?"

"There was a shooting involving Demarion Lee. He was the victim. There were three people involved all brothers. Their street names are Justice, Scoop, and Supreme. They went into rob him and ended up shooting him three times. The same three may be involved in the shooting a few weeks after that, that happened on Gladstone."

"Well how can I be sure this info is correct?"

"You're a detective I threw a dog a bone, now do some investigating. That is your job correct." Dunk said as he hung up the receiver to pay phone, got into his BMW M6 and pulled off.

Dunk grabbed the cell phone out of the cup holder and read the text messages that were sent while he was snitching to the police. He felt like a bitch that he broke the code he had kept his whole life but when he read that text, he had a shot at redemption a chance to make it right with him and the game God! So, he thought.

A few hours later Dunk and three of his niggas was stepping on a plane headed for Las Vegas. If his niggas knew what he did just a few hours ago they wouldn't be riding with him or for him. They would have rolled on him. But you never know one's intentions until everything unfolds. Part of the game is to stay on your toes Get Rich or Die Tryin. Everyone knew snitches get left in ditches.

23

Supreme justice and Milly had just exited the 95 South Freeway and into the desert, a place known for riding dirt bikes and off-roading known as Apex. They drove for another three miles on a dirt road until they spotted a black 4 x 4 Chevy truck that sat high off the ground. They pulled up in front of them and flashed the headlights on the Tahoe.

Two men got out of the truck with pistols showing on the waistband. Supreme left the truck running. Everyone got out, "I'll do the talking. y'all stay on point." Scoop said.

After they got out of the truck Scoop approached the two men as everyone else stood back far enough to scope out the scenery but close enough to hear every word said.

Scoop stuck his hand out expecting one of the men is shaking.

"You must be Scoop?"

"Yeah that's me" he said as he put his hand back.

"I spoke to Mi Familia and he told me you are a straightforward person and that I can trust you. But you know like I know we don't know each other. But mi Familia I can trust. How much are you looking to get Scoop?"

"10 kilos"

"Well, you're in luck." He snapped his fingers and another guy got out of the back of the truck with a black duffel bag and tossed it over to Scoop. The bag hit him in the chest as he tried not to stumble.

"In the bag is 25 kilos"

"I only need 10" Scoop said.

"Well now you have 25 and the price will be five hundred thousand."

"Well we only brought half of that." Scoop motioned for Supreme to bring the duffle bag.

"Oh, don't worry, you don't need any money right now. We will get it from you soon enough."

"Hold Up, this ain't how we do business. It's supposed to be the same way we discussed with Chuco."

"Well this is how the cartel does business. So, do what you need to do, and we'll be in touch soon."

Scoop looked down at the duffle bag and back up at the three guys getting back into their truck. He turned and handed the bag back to Justice and they all got back into the Tahoe and sat there for a second. They didn't know the deal they had just made locked them in to doing business with the Cartel.

Chuco knew what he was doing, now he would see if Scoop could stand up to the test. 25 kilos in a new city would tell him more than he needed to know about Supreme, Justice and Scoop.

"Let's go" Scoop said. Milli sat in the back with thoughts running thru his mind. He always heard about the Cartels, but never experienced doing business with them firsthand. He knew his cousins were plugged in with a different level of people.

Milli got out of the dope game to run hoes, and he was doing better than most people who were in the same industry as him.

He knew the twenty-five kilos were pennies to the suppliers, and to his calculations if they recon the bricks with a special blend they could turn twenty-five to fifty easy. And they could make at least thirty-six thousand a brick. If his calculations were right, he estimated one point eight million from this drop alone.

There was little said as they drove toward the spot with a duffle bag full of cocaine, and a quarter million in cash.

"So, where do we start?" Milli said "because twenty-five bricks might take a while to get off pushing out of one spot. I think it would be a smart idea if we had a spot on all sides of town. That way we corner the market and push it faster. I already got all the niggas we need"

Scoop sat back and listened. He was ready to

make a few major moves, but he couldn't figure out why the cartel didn't take the money they had with him. Maybe Chuco wanted to be in their pockets.

"Everything's together and we will get started ASAP." Scoop said.

This was after all Milli's City. He has the keys to everything now and they both knew that they needed each other. Millz a little less than Scoop, but Millie was about his paper that's how he got his name and he will be damned if he let this money pass him by. After all, he wouldn't have to get his hands dirty.

$ $ $ $ $

Chuco sat back with the phone to his ear, with his cowboy boots placed on the table as he took a puff of a cigar.

"Keep an eye on him. I know they are capable, but I need to know what kind of people they are dealing with."

He closed his cell phone, took a drink of his tequila, set the glass on the table, and went to check on his daughter who slept in the room down the hall.

He knew that he couldn't continue to live this kind of life and expect his daughter to have a normal life. There was something he was going to have to let go and whichever one he loved most was going to give him the answer to his dilemma. He kissed his daughter on the forehead and lightly stepped out of her room and pulled the door closed.

$ $ $ $ $

Two days went by and Elli pulled into the Americana Inn on Tropicana and Koval. She knocked on room number two ninety-six, and Dunk answered the door. Elli squeeze past Dunk moving ever so gracefully as the Versace dress complimented her hips. She tossed a Goyard bag on the bed and went straight to the bathroom.

She left the door open as she left her Versace dress on the floor and got into the shower. Dunk look at the figure and missed everything about her. She had lips like Nicki Minaj a waist like Daniel Harrington and an ass like Amber Rose.

Dunk looked at the bag that was on the bed and it broke his trans that he was in. He unzipped the duffel, there were several stacks of hundred-dollar bills on top of semi-automatic handguns and a fully auto submachine gun with an extended magazine.

All he could do was smile as he zipped up the bag and set it on the side of the bed. Dunk pulled back the blanket and the sheets on the second bed, as he came out of his clothes and headed for the shower. Elliot was having that effect on Dunk again. She was tired of running in circles after him but her love for him was unconditional and she was beyond loyal. He still didn't know why he took advantage of this woman, who always seem to put her life on the line for him. But she knew if he didn't get it right soon and come to his senses, she wasn't going to wait for him any longer.

Dunk stepped into the shower and got on his knees as the water splashed on his face. He pushed Elliot forward and began to eat her pussy from the back as she bent over bracing herself on the glass.

24

Milli had kept his word and came through. He acquired three different teams of his nigga's in each spot. They began to flood the whole city with pure cocaine. The money was flowing like a river and everyone was getting to the bag.

Scoop was missing Katrina, and all he could really think about was her. They were pushing a brick a day between all four spots there were no complaints. They were balling like the Golden State Warriors, and Justice was like Chef Curry when it came to stretching the coke. He easily turned twenty-five kilos into fifty and still had great product.

They had two spots where you could cop a gram or better, and the other two spots moving ounces at a time. They were really maximizing their profit. Millz turned out to be an asset.

$ $ $ $ $

Elliott was laying in the bed smoking. She had a lot on her mind. She knew who Dunk was looking for and she was caught in between a rock and a hard place. Her cousin back in Detroit had told her about the incident that she was in and barely made it out alive. If it wasn't for Scoop, she would be in a casket. Her car was riddled with bullets, and because of him Elliot's family didn't have to worry about her crazy abusive ex-boyfriend anymore.

Elliot reached into her purse and pulled out a single picture with two people on it. One of them was her cousin Lexi, and the other was Supreme laid out on the bed boo'd up. It was taken the same night that Dunk got robbed and Boo got killed. She gave the picture to Dunk and he looked at it, taking his time to remember every detail about the man in the picture.

"Who is this?" Dunk asked.

Elliot looked over at Dunk, rolled on top of him with both hands on his chest and kissed him on his lips.

"That's Supreme. One of the nigga's you are looking for."

Dunk looked closely at the picture. He remembered seeing the face before but couldn't put a finger on where. Dunk didn't ask any questions, he set the picture on the pillow next to him and began to kiss Elliott passionately.

There was a knock on the door and Elliot looked at Dunk with the sad face, but he had to answer it knowing who it already was. She rolled over off him and walk to the bathroom as he got up and answered the door.

"What's the deal?" Dunk said as he shook his boys' hand. Then walked thru the door with a blunt lit. He heard the water running in the bathroom," who's in the bathroom?"

"Elli who else?"

"Yeah? She made it here fast!" " Yeah I know, and she brought everything we need" he said as he picked up the duffle bag and set it next to Bone and dumped all the guns on the bed.

"And she came through." He picked up the Uzi with a 50 round mag hanging out of it.

"This all me right here" he said as he held it up and acted like he was aiming at someone. No Lie. Oh Yeah, but I came to tell you we should start looking for these nigga's in the club scene."

"Why would you think that?" Dunk asked already knowing his answer.

"If I was out here with a bunch of cash and Coke, I'd probably be in the strip club trying to get clients here and see sum bitches shake their ass all at the same time. Who wouldn't?"

"Yeah that makes sense. Let's see what the Livest Club and strip joints are, and that's where we'll start tonight."

Dunk pulled out a stack of hundreds and turned out three grand, then gave it to Bone.

"Take Pat and Dink, all y'all hit the mall and get something clean to wear."

"You know that's a bet!" He pocketed the cash and took the Uzi into his pants and walked out the door.

"Bone?"

"what's up?"

"Take this picture with you. Just in case you see him you know what to do."

"I got you." Bone said as he walked out of the hotel room and closed the door.

Dunk placed all the guns back into the bag and sat back on the bed as his mind raced. He didn't know if he was making the right move and hoped he would not regret it later. But he knew if he didn't move, he would be a Target back home instead of being a factor in the Motor City. He had to make an example out of these nigga's that robbed him or lose his position and respect. Revenge was inevitable currently. It was priority number one.

25

Now the trio from Detroit had the whole dessert snowing. Cocaine was flooding thru the streets of Sin City, and thanks to Milli the operation was running smoothly. He had a lot of experience managing operations, especially in the profession he was in. He knew how to manage money and people well, due to never wanting to go broke again.

Supreme was turnt up. He had money galore, and all the bitches were jockin. Especially this night they were on ten. Scoop, Supreme, and Justice treated the whole click of niggas that was Part of the operation to a VIP night out at the club inside of the Palms Hotel & Casino.

Several tables for the bottles inside of the Playboy club on the 43rd floor and the females was on dick. Some of the hood nigga's who had a hard time buying a twenty-dollar gram of Kush was now part of a million-dollar operation, and the pockets was full of cash now.

These out of town niggas came and put them on thanks to Mills, now a loyalty that was solid was finally clinched to them. Before they would let something turn sour and ruin the money, they would bust a nigga wig wide open. Jinx was natural where they came from. It was part of his everyday life, and he had no problem squeezing the trigger. But right now, it was time to party and enjoy themselves. They had a slew of women to pick from and they were enjoying every moment of this upscale Club.

After they were done partying, they headed over to the Spearmint Rhino strip club and waited for the manager to meet them at the Velvet Rope. They were about twenty deep, and everyone was feeling themselves. Too high and having a good time to notice something was off.

A black challenger pulled into the parking lot in front of the valet desk and rolled down the window.

Supreme did a double take behind him as he walked into the establishment.

"Did you see that Nigga?" Dunk asked.

"Nah" Bam Bam said.

"What's good?"

"Don't valet find a parking spot. I swear that's the nigga in the picture. It couldn't be this easy."

"What's up? are we going in?"

"Damn right. I got to go check this thing out for myself. I aint see the other two niggas', but I know they got to be in there too. So, tread carefully." Dunk said

"You don't think one of us should stay out here just in case they try to pull a stunt, do you?"

"Yeah you chill in a car and if you see anything funny text me. If anything, go down here you be ready to bust a nigga shit. Smoke anybody in the way no questions asked."

"I got you." He said as he cocked the Glock 17 and set it on the floor and began to roll a blunt. Dunk, Bone and Grip walked up to the Velvet rope and pulled out a bank roll of twenty-dollar bills and passed three of them to the bouncer. He grabbed the money and slid it into his pocket and unclipped the ropes and let them walk straight through.

Dunk walked into the club with his two boys. They scanned from left to right and made their way to the bar. They ordered three triple shots of Patron.

Bone spotted a large group of niggas' over in a VIP section with half of the women who worked in the club. They had all the strippers shaking their asses givin table dances as a confetti of money fell from the sky.

"I got a plan" Bone said.

"What's that?" Dunk said as he took a drink and held his breath trying to calm the hot feeling that was flowing down his throat.

"Let's page Scoop, Justice, and Supreme to the

front door and see if anybody in the club responds to the page" Dunk said.

"Shit. What we waitin for?"

Bone walked over to The DJ and held out a hundred-dollar bill. The DJ came over and leaned toward him.

"I got two requests. One, play that Drake: Forever, and two, page Scoop, Justice and Supreme to come over to the DJ booth."

The DJ took the money from Bone. A few seconds later the trio of names were flowing through the speakers.

$ $ $ $ $

Scoop was sipping straight out the bottle of Ace of Spades champagne. His brothers were getting dances. The whole crew was enjoying themselves. That Drake song started to play as the DJ got on the mic.

"Scoop, Supreme, and Justice you're wanted at the DJ booth Scoop, Supreme and Justice you're wanted at the DJ booth." The DJ said over the microphone. Scoop was the only person to hear the request. Justice, and Supreme was occupied with ass and titties in their face and on their lap. Scoop thought he was tripping when his name came blasting through the speaker again.

He stood up and got Supreme, and Justices attention.

"Someone is paging us to the DJ booth."

"Who you think it is?"

"I don't know! What? somebody know we're here? I'm going to send one of our niggas to go see who paged us."

"Alright keep an eye on him though." Scoop said.

Trip went to the DJ booth, he asked who paged the three names and he pointed over to the bar where three niggas was watching. He took a good look at them and made his way back over to the VIP.

"There were three guys sitting at the bar. The DJ said they paged you. They were mugging me too hard. Didn't seem right."

"Good looking lil homie" Scoop said as he slid him a Blue Face.

Scoop went over to Justice and Supreme and told them there were three guys at the bar looking for them. But when he looked toward the bar the three of them were nowhere to be found, just a few white customers and dancers.

They headed back over to VIP and decided to finish enjoying the rest of the night. Everybody went back to relax mode. Scoop felt comfortable cause he had a whole group of niggas' that relied on him to get paid. He knew he could rely on them to bust a nigga head if need be. And he would not hesitate to squeeze a trigger either if the situation called for it.

$ $ $ $ $

Dunk, Bone, and Gucci walked out of the front door as they seen three guys walking toward the bar. The whole click in VIP watched to make sure nothing jumped off.

"Did you get a good look at those three that was headed for the bar?"

"Yeah let's just chill until these niggas come out, I'm going to check them" Dunk said. They sat there with the windows rolled up smoking listening to Tupac Ambitionz Az a Ridah."

They sat in the car over an hour before a large group of niggas walked through the parking lot with a few of the strippers joining their Entourage.

"Drive by them slow" Dunk said as he stared at Scoop, as him and his boys walked to their cars.

Dunk rolled his window down as he inhaled the blunt and hung out of the car.

"What's good Scoop?" Dunk yelled out the passenger window in their direction.

Scoop turned around not expecting to see a nigga hanging out of the window aiming a gun in his direction. Scoop made eye contact just as Dunk began to squeeze the trigger sending bullets flying out of the barrel of his forty-five.

Emptying the clip as Cam drove out of the parking lot.

"Yo, turn this bitch around" Dunk yelled. They all hung out the window spraying the cars that everyone ran to. Cam drove at almost a hundred miles per hour down Industrial Road trying to get away from the club before anyone could get their license plate. They were on the freeway headed toward the hotel before they knew it.

"That was the niggas who robbed me. Why the fuck did you pull off before I seen him fall" he yelled at Cam. "I don't even know if I killed that nigga." Dunk said.

Cam Stuttered before he could get a whole word out "I, I, I seen the other nigga pullin out."

"If you seen that you should have shot him too. What the fuck you got a gun for if you ain't gone use it?" Dunk questioned.

$ $ $ $ $

Scoop turned to where he heard his name called. Feeling good and Tipsy and ready to shoot to the Suite they rented at the Planet Hollywood for the after party. When he saw a man hanging halfway out the car window, he knew something wasn't right. They locked eyes and it took a second to register who it was raising a gun in his Direction.

It didn't hit him until it was too late. "Oh shit!" Scoop said under his breath, as a flash of light came streaming out the muzzle of a gun. He tried to spin away and up his gun, but the bullets came too fast hitting their target. Scoop fell to the floor with a hole in his chest the size of a fifty-cent piece, the exit wound looked like a baseball exploded out of his back.

Supreme and Justice saw Scoop go down and they rushed over to where he was laying. Justice lifted his head off the ground as Scoop tried to speak, there was blood pouring out of his back and chest.

"Love yall" Scoop pushed out as he choked on blood.

"Ssshhhh. It's going to be okay. Call an ambulance Justice cried."

"Katrina, I love her!"

"I know, I know it's going to be okay. I'll tell her, I love you bro. Stay with us please! Stay with us." Scoop took his last breath as Supreme sat there not able to do anything.

Milli ran over there to where Scoop laid, "y'all get out of here the police on the way."

It didn't register. Millz pulled on Justice and Supreme "get out of here" Millz yelled as he gave one of his boys Scoops Pistol. "I got this."

Justice snapped back to reality. Supreme dug into Scoop's pockets and retrieved his phone money and his car keys. Took his chain from around his neck and slid his watch off his wrist. He kissed him on the forehead and just stared at him. Justice pulled Supreme by his shirt and they both got into the Tahoe and pulled off. Millz stayed on the scene as paramedics and the Metro Police arrived.

TO BE CONTINUED...

About the Author

L.J. Laura is a Las Vegas native. He is the youngest of three siblings on his mother's side of the family and was always considered the wildest. Without a solid male role model in his life he took to the streets, where he learned how to be a man.

At the age of twenty-six he was sentenced to do twelve years in prison in the State of Texas. During his bid he decided to write about some of his experiences by putting them in story form. Grit and grim from the eyes of a poverty-stricken young man. Six years later he was released from prison, and now he introduces his first novel to you. Hope you enjoy the ride…

Made in the USA
Monee, IL
06 August 2020